# I'm 16, I'm a witch, and I still have to go to school?

The holidays this year just can't get any worse! First my dad caught the flu and can't spend Christmas with me. Then, after I gave Harvey Elvis's voice for the holiday concert, every girl in school wants him—leaving me out in the cold. And when I volunteered to take Jenny's place as Santa's elf, Santa and the presents were stolen! It'll take more than a little magic to turn this horrible day into a holiday!

My name's Sabrina, and I'm sixteen. I always knew I was different, but I thought it was just because I lived with my strange aunts, Zelda and Hilda, while my divorced parents bounced around the world. Dad's in the foreign service. The *very* foreign service. He's a witch—and so am I.

I can't run to Mom—but *not* because she's currently on an archaeological dig in Peru. She's a mortal. If I set eyes on her in the next two years, she'll turn into a ball of wax. So for now, I'm stuck with my aunts. They're hanging around to show me everything I need to know about this witch business. They say all I have to do is concentrate and point. And I thought fitting in was tough!

You probably think I have superpowers. Think again! I can't turn back time and I'm on my own when it comes to love. Of course, there are some pretty neat things I *can* do—but that's where the trouble *always* begins. . . .

**Titles in Sabrina, the Teenage Witch® Pocket Books series:**

All Pocket Book titles are available by post from:
**Simon & Schuster Cash Sales, P.O. Box 29, Douglas, Isle of Man
IM99 1BQ**
Credit cards accepted. Please telephone 01624 836000,
Fax 01624 670923, Internet http://www.bookpost.co.uk
or email: bookshop@enterprise.net for details

# Sabrina The Teenage Witch®

## Santa's Little Helper

**Cathy East Dubowski**

**Based on Characters Appearing in Archie Comics**

**And based upon the television series**
**Sabrina, The Teenage Witch**
**Created for television by Nell Scovell**
**Developed for television by Jonathan Schmock**

POCKET BOOKS

LONDON · SYDNEY · NEW YORK

POCKET
B O O K S

An imprint of Simon & Schuster UK Ltd
Africa House, 64-78 Kingsway
London WC2B 6AH

A CIP catalogue record for this book is
available from the British Library

ISBN 0 671 01519 2

10

Printed by Omnia Books Limited, Glasgow

*Merry Christmas to*
*Mark & Lauren & Megan,*
*who bring magic to my life*
*every day of the year*

Santa's Little Helper

# Chapter 1

Sabrina . . ."

Sabrina was dreaming, and someone was calling her name. A muffled voice, a voice she knew.

"Sabrina—wake up . . ."

But she didn't want to wake up. She wanted to finish her lovely dream in bed, snuggled beneath the comforter where it was warm and cozy and safe. She was dreaming about Christmas morning, when she was seven or eight, long before her parents' divorce, and she wanted to grab her mother and father by the hand and run down the stairs with them to open presents under the tree. . . .

"Sabrina . . ."

She turned over and pulled the warm covers up to her chin. Maybe if she ignored the voice—

"Sabrina!"

1

Sabrina bolted upright. "I'm up, I'm up!"

Then she realized she was floating four feet off the bed.

She dropped like a stone.

"Oof!" What a rude way to wake up.

Sabrina rubbed her eyes and shoved the long, blond hair out of her face as she looked around. Her old childhood room from her dream vanished and her parents disappeared as she remembered she was in her new room in her aunts' lovely but creaky old Victorian home. Sunlight streamed through the stained glass panes of her lovely bay window, so it must be morning.

There was no one there. Had she only dreamed someone was calling her name?

She swung her feet over the side of the bed. *Yikes! Ice-cold floors in winter are part of the price of charm in these old houses,* she thought as she knelt to search under the bed for her slippers.

"Sabri—*Cough! Cough!* Sabrina! Are you awake?"

Sabrina's eyes darted to the desk by her bed. The huge book on her desk was . . . coughing?

But, of course, this was not your ordinary paperback checked out from the library. The large leather-bound, gem-encrusted book with *The Discovery of Magic* engraved on the cover in gold looked like something you'd see in a medieval museum. Her father had given her the ancient book for her sixteenth birthday—the day she'd discovered something very special about herself.

2

Sabrina was a witch. A teenage witch.

Not only that, her father was a witch.

And the aunts she'd come to live with in the sleepy New England town of Westbridge—Zelda and Hilda Spellman, her dad's sisters. They were witches, too.

That was the day she'd found out the *real* reason she'd come to live with her aunts: so they could teach her the ancient secrets of how to use her new magic powers.

At first, Sabrina had refused to believe it. She'd thought the whole story was just one big, goofy birthday joke they'd invented to help put her at ease for her first day at a new school—especially when her aunts gave her a fat, black cauldron for a present.

What had convinced her that she and her aunts and her father were really witches? Maybe it was when snobby cheerleader Libby Chessler had called her a freak and spilled a drink on her that first day of school—and Sabrina had gotten so mad she'd blasted the cafeteria full of thunder and lightning and turned Libby into a pineapple just by pointing her finger at the girl.

Or maybe it was when she first heard Salem—the black American shorthair cat that lived with her aunts—speak English. Sarcastically.

But what finally convinced her was when she looked in that ancient *The Discovery of Magic* book and saw a black-and-white engraving of a handsome man dressed in a black top hat, tuxedo, and cape—a man who looked an awful lot like her dad.

Too much like her dad.

"Surprise! It *is* your dad!" the man in the picture had announced cheerfully as he shimmered to life. "Happy birthday, Sabrina!"

She had totally freaked out. All her life she'd thought her dad was traveling with the foreign service—it was just a lot more *foreign* than she'd realized.

But then she'd chilled a little, and her father and aunts had explained to her that there were two realms of existence—the natural and the supernatural—and that, as a young witch, she could now experience life in both worlds.

Of course, she had to go through the upstairs linen closet to get to some of those places in the supernatural realm. But she could deal with that.

In fact, once she'd accepted the idea that she was half-witch and there was nothing she could do about it, she'd discovered that having magic powers was actually pretty cool.

Only it didn't make life perfect. She couldn't use her magic to get rid of zits, reverse her parents' divorce, or make Harvey Kinkle fall in love with her. But that was okay. She'd done a pretty good job of that all by herself.

And, of course, she still had to go to high school.

School! She'd better get up and get going. Time

was another thing her witch powers couldn't fool around with.

"Sabrina," someone rasped from between the parchment pages. "Open the book—*cough, cough.* I need to—*cough*—talk to you."

It sounded like her dad!

Quickly Sabrina picked up the huge book from her desk, propped it up on the pillows of her bed, and flipped open to the page she always kept marked with the volume's red satin bookmark.

Edward Spellman's face shimmered to life. *"A-choo!"*

"Dad!" Sabrina said worriedly. "Are you all right?"

"Yes, honey, I'm fi—fi—*fa-choo!"* Her father blew his nose on a silk handkerchief and then looked up from the pages of the book with bleary eyes. He was a handsome man, with thick, black hair and a usually charming smile. But this morning he looked awful. "Actually, to tell you the truth, I'm not fine. I feel terrible!"

"What's wrong?" Sabrina asked, then, with a sudden thought, leaned back from the book. "And can I catch it?"

"Not from an image in the book," her father reassured her.

Sabrina relaxed, but she was still worried about her father. He almost never got sick. "What have you got?" she asked. "A cold or something?"

"I wish," her father muttered, then sputtered quickly as his image began to sparkle:

5

*"Cancel the wish mine lips have spoken!
By clapping thrice mine spell be broken!"*

He clapped three times, coughing as he did, then ran a shaky hand through his thick, dark hair. "Whew, that was close. I certainly don't need a cold on top of everything else!"

"But you're sneezing," Sabrina noted. "And coughing, too. If it's not a cold, what is it?"

Edward rubbed his aching forehead. "I've got the Witch's Blue Flu."

"Why do they call it the Blue Flu?" Sabrina asked.

"You'd know if you could see me in person," the black-and-white drawing of her father said. "I'm all blue!"

*"Ewww,* sounds awful," Sabrina said. "So can't you take a pill or say a spell or something and get better?"

"I'm afraid there's only one cure for the Witch's Blue Flu."

"What's that?"

"Time. I've just got to wait it out."

A stab of fear shot through Sabrina's heart. "But . . . you'll be better soon, right?" she asked him. "Like, in time for Christmas?"

Sabrina didn't need to hear him speak. She saw his answer in the painful look that filled his dark brown eyes.

"I'm sorry, sweetheart," Edward told his daughter. "I'm afraid I won't be well for weeks. I'd give

6

anything not to be sick. I know how much you've always loved Christmas."

"So, just come anyway," Sabrina insisted. "I don't care if you're sick—I can look after you! I can bring you food and Tylenol and read to you and—"

"No, Sabrina," her father interrupted. "The Witch's Blue Flu is extremely contagious to witches in person. And it's especially rough on teenagers."

"But, Dad, I don't care—"

"Well, I do, Sabrina. I don't want to risk it. This is a really awful illness, and I couldn't bear to infect you with it. I know you're disappointed, sweetheart, but there's nothing I can do. I'm sure you'll have fun with Zelda and Hilda."

"But I want to be with you and Mom!" Sabrina cried.

Sabrina winced at the pained look that crossed her father's face. Edward Spellman could give his daughter practically anything in the cosmos.

But not that.

Sabrina's mom was a gifted archaeologist—a one-hundred-percent *mortal* archaeologist—and she was off digging up ancient vases and other miscellaneous cracked artifacts in the South American country of Peru. She loved her work and was dedicated to her current research—but that wasn't why she'd left Sabrina behind.

There was this rule, her father had explained to Sabrina that day she'd learned she was truly a witch. Once Sabrina came into her powers on her sixteenth birthday, she couldn't set eyes on her mortal mother during the next two years or her mom would . . . well, her mom would turn into a big ball of wax.

Permanently.

Not good.

Her father had explained that it was one of the rules the authorities in the supernatural realm used to discourage mortal-witch marriages. And even though her parents were divorced now, the rule still applied to Sabrina's relationship with her mother.

Since she knew there was no way to spend Christmas with her mother, she'd been counting on spending the holidays with her dad.

Sabrina—who was usually a pretty upbeat kind of girl—felt her mood plummet.

"So I get to spend Christmas all alone—like some kind of orphan?" Sabrina complained, her eyes burning with a sudden flash of hot tears. She knew it was a mean, unfair thing to say, but she felt so rotten, she didn't care.

"Sabrina, you're not an orphan," her father said, a bit sharp himself. "You have two parents who love you more than you can imagine. And what about Zelda and Hilda?"

"It's not the same," Sabrina complained.

"Look, Sabrina," her father said more gently, "I know this is a difficult time in your life, you're

8

going through a lot of changes, and I wish I could be there for you more often than I am. But getting sick is part of life—even a witch's life—and there's nothing we can do about it now but make the best of it. Right?"

"I guess . . ."

"I promise, when I'm better"—Edward stopped to deal with another coughing fit—"I promise we'll have our own Christmas celebration. What do you say?"

*Great,* Sabrina thought. *Christmas on St. Patrick's Day. Can't wait.*

But she knew it wasn't her father's fault that he was sick, so she tried to give him a great big smile. "Okay, Dad. I understand."

Edward smiled in relief. "That's my girl. Now—a-*choo!*—I guess I'd better go and get some rest. If you need me, you'll find me listed under *Q*."

"*Q?*" Sabrina asked, puzzled. "How come?"

"For 'Quarantine,'" her father explained. "This stuff's so contagious, they've got a whole separate chapter in the back of the book for all us sick folk."

"So there's somebody there to look after you?" Sabrina asked.

"Yeah, I'll be fine. And don't worry. I'll probably sleep through most of it."

"Okay, Dad. I hope you feel better."

"Thanks—*cough, cough.* Well, good-bye, sweetheart." Then, as his image began to flatten on the page once more, he called out, *"Promise me you'll drink your orange juice, Sabrina! And that you'll wear your mittens when you go outsiiiiiiiide. . . ."*

"I'll try!" Sabrina hollered back, which was the best she could promise. And then, suddenly sorry she'd been so grouchy with her father when he was sick, she shouted, "I love you, Dad!"

But Edward Spellman's image had already disappeared from the page of other *S* words with a soft little *poof.*

Sabrina closed the huge leather book and carried it to her desk, where she laid it beside her red lava lamp. It could be worse, she supposed. She knew some kids whose parents were divorced, and some of them never even saw their dads at all. She pulled out the book's red satin bookmark and used it to mark the *Q*'s.

She grinned. At least she knew where to find her father if she needed him!

"Sabrina!" she heard her aunt Zelda call from downstairs. "If you're going to school, better get a move on!"

Maybe if she wore something Christmasy to school it would cheer her up. Shivering in her long, white nightgown, she tiptoed across the cold, wooden floorboards and stared at herself in her full-length mirror, thinking, then *snap!* Her white nightgown instantly changed into a green turtleneck, red leather mini, and knee-high black boots.

"Oh, brother," she muttered. "I look like one of

Santa's elves!" She snapped again, and zapped the entire outfit black. *Hmmm, all I need now is a motorcycle,* she thought, but the somber color suited her mood, so she decided to stick with it. After waving her hand to make her hairbrush magically stroke through her long, blond hair, banishing all her tangles, she grabbed her backpack and headed down the stairs to breakfast.

Her aunts were sitting at the kitchen table, sipping café au lait.

Both were attractive, with short, blond hair, but Aunt Zelda was elegant and graceful, a true intellectual as well as a dreamer. Aunt Hilda was hipper, and a bit more childish, with a dimple that showed whenever she grinned.

Aunt Zelda's reading glasses slipped down her nose as she typed something into her laptop computer.

Aunt Hilda was reading her daily horoscope on the newspaper's comics page.

Salem the cat sat next to a saucer of half-and-half, frowning miserably as he studied the financial news. The Witches' Council had turned him into a cat for a hundred years as punishment for plotting to take over as world emperor. By carefully playing the stocks, he planned to be so wealthy by the time they changed him back, he wouldn't care *who* ruled the world.

Sabrina sat down and zapped herself a quick bowl of Frosted Happy-O's. Much to her disappointment, she had learned early on that witches couldn't do name brands, but these were nearly as good.

"Sabrina, what's wrong?" Zelda asked as she watched her niece mope over her bowl of cold cereal. "You look like you just lost your best friend."

"I didn't lose him," Sabrina replied. "He's just not coming for Christmas."

"Are you talking about your father?" Zelda asked.

Sabrina nodded sadly as she floated a small juice glass from the kitchen cupboard to the table. "He just called me from the book." She pointed at her glass and zapped it full of orange juice.

"Ted's not coming?" Hilda asked with a worried frown. "Is he sick or something?"

"The Witch's Blue Flu," Sabrina said.

Her aunts both gasped.

"That's awful!" Hilda exclaimed. "I had the worst case of the Witch's Blue Flu on February 9, 1964."

"You remember the exact date?" Sabrina asked.

Hilda nodded. "I was *so* sick! They put me in Quarantine, and I had to miss The Beatles' first appearance on *The Ed Sullivan Show.* I was so bummed!"

"How long did yours last?" Sabrina asked her aunt.

Hilda thought a minute. "Till 'I Want to Hold

Your Hand' dropped on the charts to number three. I thought I'd be sick *forever!*"

Zelda removed her glasses and closed her laptop. "I'll have to call him," she said, shaking her head. "Ted was always such a baby when he got sick when we were little. He'll be miserable." She chuckled as she got up to look into her wooden spice cabinet, which actually contained many of the mysterious ingredients that the Spellman sisters used to concoct potions and brews. "Maybe I'll make him some of Mama's special homemade chicken soup. . . . Now, let's see. Hilda, did you use all the powdered chicken's beak?"

Sabrina just shrugged and returned to staring into her bowl of soggy cereal.

After removing a few dusty glass vials from the spice cabinet, Zelda turned toward the cupboards, but stopped when she noticed Sabrina propping her head on one hand and stirring mindless circles in her cereal with the other. "Hmm," Zelda said, tapping her lips with one long finger. "Young lady, I think you need something more substantial than a soggy bowl of sugar on a cold morning like this. Something that will stick to your ribs—" She pointed her finger and—*Zap!*

Sabrina's Happy-O's turned into mush. As in hot, steaming oatmeal.

Sabrina frowned. "But I want Happy-O's." She zapped it back.

*"Oatmeal is more nutritious."* ZAP!

13

*"Happy-O's!"*

*"Oatmeal!"*

*"Happy-O's!"* Sabrina pointed at the now spinning bowl, but this time nothing happened. "Hey!" she cried, staring at her malfunctioning digit. "What's wrong with my finger?"

Aunt Zelda brushed off her hands in triumph. "Nothing. I just outzapped you. It's a privilege of age. Now, eat! We don't want you getting sick like your father."

Sabrina made a face, but dug into the warm, cinnamony oatmeal, which was actually the most delicious oatmeal she'd ever tasted. Who needed that Quaker guy when her aunt could cook like this?

"So," Hilda said brightly, folding the newspaper. "I guess it'll just be us three for the holidays."

Salem loudly cleared his throat. "Hel-*lo.*"

"Did I say three?" Hilda asked. "What was I thinking?"

"Three, four, two-hundred-and-twenty . . ." Sabrina mumbled. "Who cares?"

"What did you say, Sabrina dear?" Zelda asked. "Nothing."

"Maybe we could get a tree or something," Zelda suggested brightly.

Sabrina shrugged. "Yeah, maybe." Her aunts were both really cool, but they were much more into Halloween than Christmas. And they didn't have kids of their own, so how could they possibly understand how Sabrina felt? Her chair screeched on the floor as she got up, took her bowl to the sink, then hurried to the hall closet to get her down coat. "I gotta go. See you." Dragging her backpack and slipping one arm into her coat, she plodded out the door.

*Merry Christmas? Bah, humbug.* It was going to be the worst one ever.

As the door slammed, her aunts exchanged a worried glance.

# Chapter 2

☆

*At least I've got my friends,* Sabrina thought as she climbed off the bus and headed into the sprawling two-story redbrick building that was Westbridge High School.

As she hurried inside to her locker, she heard her least favorite person—Libby Chessler—squealing about something as a large crowd of kids gathered round her in the hall. Sabrina tried not to listen, but who could help it? Libby wasn't head cheerleader for nothing. She had a big mouth.

Sabrina shook her head. Libby was pretty, with glossy dark hair and a slim figure that was always draped in the latest expensive fashion. She was also snobby, rude, and extremely conceited. But for some strange reason she was probably the most popular girl in school, and wielded power over all the dozens of lesser nobodies who wandered the halls, hoping to be part of her crowd. *Go figure,* Sabrina thought. Who wrote the rules for this popularity system? How come *nice* never figured into the equation?

And for some reason Libby had had it in for Sabrina ever since that first day of school. Maybe it had something to do with the fact that Sabrina and Harvey had hit it off. Libby didn't like to lose.

"Sabrina," Libby called as she and her crowd of admirers flowed down the hall. "Did you see the latest issue of *Beautiful Living New England?*" She held up the cover of the glossy home-decor magazine as if she were one of those game-show models displaying a prize.

"Gosh, Libby, no," Sabrina said sarcastically as she opened her locker. "I guess my subscription ran out."

Libby ignored the barb and gushed, "You've just *got* to see it—because *I'm* in it!" She flipped open the magazine and shoved it in front of Sabrina's face. "Here—see? It's this issue's main story, all about *me*—well, and my family—and our beautiful house, all decorated for the holidays. Look— the editors called it 'The *Perfect* Christmas.' Isn't that just . . . *so* perfect?"

Sabrina stared at the two-page color photograph at the beginning of the story. Libby and her family, dressed in beautiful holiday outfits, smiled serenely from their pose before a crackling fire.

"Hey, Libby," Harvey said, coming up behind

Sabrina to peer at the magazine. "Your house looks really cool."

"Thanks, Harvey," Libby said with a smug smile, batting her thick eyelashes. "You're welcome to come over and see it for yourself anytime."

Harvey grinned. "Well, thanks. That's really nice of you. But, hey, I didn't know you had a golden retriever. Is it new?"

"Oh, that." Libby chuckled, but Sabrina noticed a slight blush stain her cheeks. "She's not ours. The magazine crew thought a dog would add a nice touch to the photo spread—you know how they do these things—so they had Daphne's Golden Duchess brought in. Isn't she gorgeous? She's won dozens of blue ribbons at competitions," she added, as proudly as if the dog were hers.

"How about the parents?" Sabrina asked dryly. "Did they bring them in, too?"

"Of course not!" Libby retorted. "They're real." Then her frown melted as she stepped between Sabrina and Harvey. "By the way, Harvey, I'm having a few dozen close friends over this afternoon for a tour and an autograph-signing with light refreshments. Want to come?"

"That sounds like fun." Harvey turned to Sabrina. "What do you think, Sabrina? Want to go?"

He didn't see the murderous look Libby shot Sabrina. One that quite plainly said, *You're* so *not invited.*

Sabrina fought the urge to turn Libby into a sprig of mistletoe. Libby, who kept an alphabetical list of all the hearts she'd broken, had set her sights on Harvey just about the time Sabrina had arrived at Westbridge. But Harvey was so sweet and thought so well of people that he never seemed to see what a creep Libby was. "She's always been nice to me," he'd say with a shrug.

But Libby seemed unable to accept that Sabrina was dating a guy that she'd wanted to add to her list. Like the spoiled little rich girl that she was, she wanted what she couldn't have.

Sabrina shrugged. "Thanks, but . . . I don't think so."

"So, Sabrina," Libby asked loudly. "What are *you* doing for Christmas?"

For some reason, everyone seemed to stop talking right at that moment. She felt a thousand eyes on her as she answered, "Um, spending it with my aunts."

"Without your parents?" Libby said, her voice dripping with pity. "I'm so sorry."

*Too bad you're not spending Christmas at the* real *North Pole,* Sabrina thought, her temper flaring; her fingers just itched to send her there, air mail. But she stuffed her hands into the pockets of her black leather mini just in time and instead replied, "Hey, I'm not. My aunts are the greatest!"

"So, what are you doing?" Libby asked, refusing to let her off the hook.

Sabrina glanced around at the expectant faces. So what was this, the witness stand? Sabrina opted for, "It's a surprise. My aunts love to surprise me."

"Well, have fun," Libby said in a voice that said she was sure Sabrina wouldn't, then continued down the hall with her magazine. "Hey, Mitchell, have you seen the latest issue of *Beautiful Living New England . . . ?*"

Sabrina turned back to her locker with a scowl on her face. So who cared whether some lame magazine posed Libby's family like a bunch of Barbie dolls and called it perfect? She wouldn't change places with Libby for all the CDs in the world.

"I never met anyone who was in a magazine before," Harvey said as he leaned against the lockers. "Have you?" Just then he dropped a brown paper grocery bag on the floor, and Sabrina bent to pick it up.

"Don't!" Harvey shouted, and snatched the bag out of her grasp.

"Uh, sorry," Sabrina said, taken aback. "Didn't mean to touch your bag." She tried making a joke. "That's a pretty big lunch you've got there."

"Oh, it's not my lunch," he said, but didn't explain. He stuffed the bag into his backpack. "I gotta go."

Just then her best friend, Jenny Kelly, ran up, her long, curly red hair flying out behind her like a banner. "Am I late? My parents and I were up late last night baking for the holidays. We didn't get to bed till two A.M."

*Rriiiiiiiiiing!*

"You just made it," Sabrina reassured her.

Together they hurried off to class.

In homeroom during morning announcements, Libby's cheery voice came on the intercom. "The cheerleaders of Westbridge High School—of which I am the head—are sponsoring a Wish Tree at the Westbridge Mall this holiday season. We'd like to urge every student at school to donate at least one new toy to give to underprivileged children in our area. I guess . . . unless, of course, *you're* underprivileged, and then I guess we invite you to feel free to put your name on a sign-up sheet on the main bulletin board, and we'll see about sending toys to your house, too."

Sabrina couldn't believe the things that Libby said sometimes. "Since when is she into charity projects?" Sabrina whispered to Jenny. "I thought she hated volunteer work."

Jenny giggled. "Didn't you read the article in *Beautiful Living New England?*"

"Nope, missed that one. But Libby showed us this morning."

"Well," Jenny went on, "her mother and father went on and on in the interview about the responsibility of the privileged to give something back at Christmastime, and how one of their family's biggest Christmas traditions is that they each have a favorite holiday charity."

"So that's it," Sabrina said.

"If anyone is interested in volunteering to help with the project," Libby went on, "please sign up on the main bulletin board and I'll give you a call. Thanks, and Go, Fighting Scallions!"

That was the name of the Westbridge sports team. Originally they were supposed to be the Fighting Stallions, but a typo at the printer's had changed all that. They'd gone from fighting horses to fighting vegetables. Their colors were green and white. Just like scallions. Their Consumers Class teacher always tried to tell them how clever it was, since, of course, eating vegetables made you strong. But eating scallions just gave you strong breath. And since the tiny white onions with the long green stalks were somewhere on the cafeteria menu every day, Sabrina always made sure she carried some mints in her bag.

Sabrina's classes spun by in a blur. The teachers didn't bother to teach much, since most of the kids were too excited about getting out for holiday break to pay much attention. Sabrina spent most of the day listening to everyone else's cheerful banter about their Christmas or Hanukkah or Kwanzaa plans. A lot of people were traveling to visit relatives, to places like California, New York, Charlotte, even England. Sabrina wondered what it was like in Peru this time of year.

At lunchtime she and Jenny sat at their usual table engrossed in their usual lunchtime pastime: trying to figure out what the food on their tray was supposed to be.

"I think this is supposed to be turkey and dressing," Jenny said, poking at the gravy-drenched mass.

"But it's green!" Sabrina protested.

"Food coloring?" Jenny suggested with a shrug. "Or maybe scallion tops?"

"Well, I'm not eating green meat, even for Christmas," Sabrina said.

Just then Sabrina spotted Harvey buying milk at the end of the lunch line and waved him over.

"Uh, hi, Sabrina," he said nervously as he stopped by their table. But instead of a cafeteria tray, he was holding a bag lunch.

"Can't face the green turkey, huh?" Sabrina said.

"Um, actually, I can't eat in the cafeteria today," Harvey said. "I've got something I've got to do."

"Oh." Sabrina smiled, waiting for him to explain. But he didn't.

"Well, I guess I'll see you guys later," he said.

"Sure. Later."

Sabrina's smile faded as she watched Harvey disappear down the hall. She and Harvey and Jenny had rarely missed eating lunch together since her first day at Westbridge High. She couldn't help but wonder what he had to do that was so important he would skip lunch.

". . . and I'm just so excited!" Jenny was saying.

"Hmm?"

"About all my relatives coming," Jenny said. "This is like the biggest family reunion my family has ever had, and it is so cool we get to have it at my house. Both my parents are from large families, and I've got relatives coming from everywhere. Some of them I haven't seen in years. Even my great-grandmother Irene will be there, and she's ninety-two. Can you believe it?"

*If you think your grandmother's old,* Sabrina thought with a grin, *you ought to see my aunts' birth certificates!*

Jenny cautiously tasted her cherry cobbler. "Huh. Not bad. You should taste it. Anyway, my mom and I are going to be majorly busy getting ready for everybody. She's been cooking for days. I wish I didn't have to work, too."

Sabrina remembered that Jenny had gotten a part-time job at the mall, working as an elf helping with the little kids who wanted to sit on Santa's lap.

"How's your job going?" Sabrina asked, skipping the cobbler in favor of her roll. Bread was difficult even for the cafeteria to ruin.

"Not bad," Jenny said. "The only bad part is that I was really looking forward to hanging out with you some during the holidays. But it looks like I'm not going to have any free time at all."

"Bummer," Sabrina said.

*Maybe I should just spend the holidays skiing on Mars,* Sabrina grumbled. *Nah, did that for Thanksgiving.*

Besides, spending Christmas away from home just wouldn't be the same.

That afternoon Sabrina said good-bye to Jenny,

who was off to work at the mall, and went to meet
Harvey at their lockers, as usual.

She found him pulling that big, crumpled paper
bag from his locker and tapped him on the
shoulder.

"So, no basketball practice this afternoon, huh?"
Sabrina asked.

"Nope. No Scallions till after New Year's," he
said.

"So, want to go sledding in the park or something?"

Harvey's eyes, usually so open and honest,
shifted uneasily. "Uh, sorry, Sabrina. I'd really
love to, but I can't. Not today."

"How come?"

"I, uh, I'm sort of busy."

"Oh." Sabrina dropped her gaze. She wouldn't
allow herself to say *Busy doing what?* But her
silence seemed to make Harvey nervous, and instead of leaving it at that, he rushed to fill in an
explanation.

"I, um, promised my mom I'd help her bake
Christmas cookies this afternoon," he said.

*Oh, Harvey,* Sabrina thought, *you're a terrible
liar.*

"Oh." Sabrina nodded. "That sounds really
nice." She smiled expectantly, hoping maybe, just
maybe, he really was going home to bake cookies
and that maybe, just maybe, he'd invite her to join
them.

25

But he didn't.

In fact, he seemed really eager to get away from her. Surely it was her imagination.

"Well, gotta go," he said with a self-conscious shrug.

Sabrina's heart twisted. And then he dashed down the hallway and out into the cold afternoon.

Instead of taking the bus, she walked home in the snow that still lay on the ground from last week's snowstorm. Everywhere she looked it seemed she saw families or friends or couples experiencing some holiday Kodak moment. Maybe they were filming a Hallmark commercial in Westbridge and they'd just forgotten to tell her.

She was feeling pretty left out.

"Hey, kid, want to buy a Christmas tree?"

Sabrina glanced up at a tall, skinny guy in a blue knit stocking cap. He and his short buddy stood next to a big truck parked on the side of the road.

"Maybe," she said. She could take it home and get her aunts to help decorate it. They could string popcorn and sing Christmas carols. Maybe that would help it feel like Christmas.

But then she looked in the back of the guys' truck. Gross! The trees were skimpy and twisted and missing half their needles. The ones that still clung to the branches were quickly turning brown. "Are these left over from last year or what?" Sabrina said, walking away. "Thanks, but no thanks."

"Hey, you'll be sorry, missy!" the tall, skinny guy called out. "Best price in town."

*That's all I need to cheer me up,* she thought grumpily, *a half-dead Christmas tree.*

As she wandered on home, she wondered about Harvey.

Harvey was such a sweet guy. Nice. Straightforward. Maybe not the most *observant* guy sometimes. But a good guy. Really honest and true-blue.

So why did Sabrina get the strong feeling that he wasn't being completely honest with *her?*

*Is he hiding something?* she wondered.

Maybe he was heading over to Libby's "Perfect Christmas" thing and just didn't want to hurt her feelings.

Or even worse—

Was he trying to give her the *brush-off* for Christmas?

☆

# Chapter 3

☆

Sabrina winced and covered her face with her cold hands.

She had walked home from school in the snow, alone—since everyone seemed busy with some fabulous holiday event or other that they just *had* to go to and just *couldn't* include her in.

So she was cold and feeling lonesome and looking forward to a good helping of sympathy—and maybe something chocolate—from her aunts.

But a half-block from home she couldn't believe what she saw.

That *wasn't* her aunts' house.

No way.

*Couldn't* be.

She peeked through her freezing fingers.

It was.

Either that, or the Spellman sisters' entire Vic-

torian house at 133 Collins Road had been replaced by a time-traveling disco Christmas party
from 1977.

"If the Bee Gees are in there doing the Holiday
Hustle with Aunt Hilda and Aunt Zelda, I'm out of
here," Sabrina mumbled as she stared in disbelief.

The house pulsed with a million neon lights. Up
on the rooftop, a chorus line of flashing Reindeer
Rockettes kicked up their hooves. Next to that, an
animated Santa perched on the chimney, clutching his round belly and shouting, "Ho, Ho, Ho,
Mer-r-r-r-ry Christmas!" over . . . and *over* . . .
and *over* . . . .

From top to bottom, every window, turret, door,
and gutter was outlined in blinking Christmas
lights—so was every tree, bush, and weed in the
yard. A life-size plastic snowman glowed in the
twilight near an automated Santa's workshop with
hammering, humming elves.

Unfortunately, her aunts had gone a bit heavy on
their favorite holiday colors—orange and black—
which made the place look a little like Halloween at
the North Pole.

Flashing four-foot plastic candy canes lined the
curving sidewalk leading up to the big old-
fashioned porch, where the old wooden door was
completely covered with orange foil gift wrap, with
a big, black bow the size of a dinner plate stuck in
the middle.

Above the door spun a silvery disco ball that sent

tiny gemlike lights dancing across the porch. But instead of disco music, it was accompanied by a scratchy holiday recording of Burl Ives singing very loudly, "Have a Holly Jolly Christmas."

Sabrina winced as she watched a man and a woman cover their ears and hurry past on the sidewalk.

Mortified, Sabrina ran up the steps and onto the front porch, and nearly shrieked when she stepped on the poinsettia doormat, which activated a recording of a Boris Karloff-like rendition of "The Monster Mash."

Sabrina grabbed the doorknob and shoved her way into the entry hall of the usually cozy Spellman home. Once inside, she looked around the living room and groaned.

It looked like Mrs. Claus's yard sale.

A revolving color wheel drenched the ten-foot-tall white artificial Christmas tree in a twirling pattern of red and green light, glinting off the multitude of gold and silver ornaments.

On the kitchen counters several bowls of batter stirred themselves, while a rolling pin rolled out cookie dough. The kitchen table was piled high with fruitcakes. *I hate fruitcake*, Sabrina groaned. *What are those weird green things anyway?*

In the living room, Aunt Zelda was setting up several of those light-up collectible villages into a major metropolitan area on the coffee table. Salem was busy chasing a tiny electric train around the base of the tree. Aunt Hilda was leaping around spraying everything with a can of fake snow.

Sabrina dropped her backpack to the floor and let the door slam shut behind her.

"Sabrina!" Aunt Zelda exclaimed, startled. "You're home!"

She and Hilda hurried over to greet their niece.

"Surprise!" they both shouted.

Sabrina bit her lip. The look on her aunts' faces nearly broke her heart—they were obviously proud of the outlandish decorating they'd done.

They'd gone totally overboard.

And the worst part? Sabrina knew they'd done it all for her.

"So—how do you like it?" Hilda asked, dimpling as she grinned like a delighted little girl.

Sabrina forced a smile to her lips as she dragged off her down coat. "Wow . . ."

Zelda clapped her hands. "Are you surprised?"

"Surprised . . . ?" Sabrina nodded. *"Floored."*

"Don't you just love it?" Hilda demanded cheerfully.

Sabrina's cheeks turned red as her aunts stood side by side, staring at her, waiting for her to just love it.

"I . . ." She was trying to love it, she really was. But she couldn't force those words to her lips. "Surprised," she repeated enthusiastically, hoping that would do. "I'm *definitely* surprised."

Zelda's and Hilda's smiles faded.

31

*Uh-oh.* "Really, it's totally outrageous!" Sabrina tried.

The aunts crossed their arms and narrowed their startling eyes at their niece.

"Sabrina . . ." Zelda said in that quiet, firm voice of hers that said, *I'm not buying it, buster!*

*Think fast,* Sabrina told herself. *Say something—anything—nice.* "Um, I'm . . . sure the electric bill will make the utility company really happy?"

Her aunts' faces fell.

*Oops. Bad answer.*

Her aunts looked at each other.

"She doesn't like it," Zelda said with a sigh.

"She hates it," Hilda agreed with a pout.

"No, really—"

But her aunts ignored her. Shoulder to shoulder, their mouths set in a grim line, they snapped their fingers.

*Whooooosh!* A blast of cold air tousled Sabrina's hair and sent goose bumps down her spine as it whisked through the living room, and instantly every last ornament, every sprig of greenery, every sprinkle of sparkly snow disappeared from the Spellman living room.

"Hey!" Salem whined as the train caboose disappeared from beneath his paw. "I wasn't through with that!"

Aiming out the bay window, Hilda wound up her arm like a baseball pitcher, and—

*Poof!* The outdoor lights, the candy canes, the

snowman—and no doubt Santa and his rooftop Reindeer Rockettes—vanished.

All except the silvery disco ball. The front door opened, and the ball—still spinning and bathing the room in its sparkling lights—floated into the entry hall and up the stairs to the second floor.

Hilda shrugged. "I always wanted one of those."

Sabrina plopped down on the comfortable couch with a contrite look on her face. "Aunt Zelda, Aunt Hilda, I'm sorry—"

"No, Sabrina, *we're* sorry," Aunt Zelda said softly as she and Hilda sat down on either side of her like bookends. "I was afraid we'd get it all wrong."

"We weren't sure what look to go for," Hilda explained. "So we sort of did them all. I was just having so much fun." She added gleefully, "You should have seen what I had planned for the backyard—"

Zelda laid a hand on her bubbly sister's arm and shook her head.

Hilda sighed. "I guess we went a little overboard, huh?"

Sabrina grinned and held up her thumb and forefinger. "Maybe just a *teensy* bit . . ."

"You know we were just trying to make it nice for you, sweetheart," Aunt Zelda said.

"I know . . ."

"I know it must be hard, not seeing your mom and dad for Christmas," Zelda said. "But we'll be glad to do whatever you want to make this Christmas as special as those you had when you were growing up."

Sabrina shrugged. "That's just the trouble, Aunt Zelda. I don't know *what* I want. It just seems as if everyone is enjoying the holiday season but me. I mean, Jenny's got all these relatives coming——"

"We're relatives," Zelda reminded her.

"Relatively speaking," Salem commented.

"And Harvey's baking cookies with his mom——"

"Cookies! I can get into that," Hilda said. She zapped a plate of warm, delicious-smelling cookies—assorted varieties—onto the coffee table. She selected three, then used her finger to levitate the plate to Sabrina.

Sabrina stuffed a gingerbread boy into her mouth. "Am Wibby's bwagging——"

"Don't talk with your mouth full, dear," Zelda quietly reminded. She took her job of raising a well-mannered young witch very seriously.

"Um, sowwy." Sabrina snapped her fingers, and a glass of milk appeared. After taking a drink to wash down the cookie crumbs, she continued. "And Libby's going around bragging because her family is in *Beautiful Living New England* magazine in a decorating photo spread called 'The Perfect Christmas.'"

Hilda rubbed her chin. "Hmmm, I don't know a single witch in the magazine business. How about you, Zelda?"

"Well, I do know the editor of *Quantum Physics*

*Bimonthly,*" Zelda said thoughtfully. "But I'm afraid their Christmas issue is already out." She picked up the publication from the coffee table to show them.

"That's okay," Hilda said, snatching the thick magazine from her sister's hands. "I can fix that." She mumbled a few words, thumped the cover with a glitzy nail, then flipped through the glossy pages. "Ah, here it is. Page 46. What do you think?" She held it out for Sabrina to see.

Sabrina gasped in surprise. A black-and-white photo showed Sabrina and her aunts wearing long, velvet dresses as they sipped tea and chatted with a bearded gentleman before a roaring fire.

Sabrina peered at the small book that the man was reading. *A Christmas Carol* by Charles Dickens, it said in neat lettering. "Who's that guy?" she asked.

"Charles Dickens," Hilda replied.

"You mean *the* Charles Dickens?" Sabrina exclaimed.

"Yeah," Hilda replied dreamily. "Chuck was such a cute guy! And *crazy*. Too bad he was married. I love a guy who can tell a good ghost story."

"But how'd you do that?" Sabrina asked. "I never met Charles Dickens. I wasn't even born yet!"

Hilda shrugged. "I just airbrushed you in. What do you think?"

Zelda grabbed the magazine back and glared at

her sister. "Hilda, how many times have I told you, you can't just go around erasing people's scientific research whenever—"

"Aw, who reads that junk anyway?" Hilda said. "I think it's the stuffiest, most boring—"

"Well, *I* do for one," Zelda shot back. "And lots of other fascinating, intelligent, inquiring people—"

Hilda laughed out loud. "Stuffed shirts and old fogies—"

"Uh-oh, catfight!" Salem said, and dashed toward the stairs. "I'm outta here."

"Guys, guys!" Sabrina stuck her hands up to separate the two squabbling siblings. Like any two sisters, they often disagreed, and it tickled Sabrina that sometimes her guardians scrapped like a couple of little girls on the playground. Only they'd been doing it since before the Middle Ages!

"It's not about my picture being in a magazine," Sabrina insisted.

"Fine," Hilda said, crossing her arms and looking away.

"Fine," Zelda agreed. With a shake of her head she zapped the original article back into the magazine.

"And it's not about cookies, either," Sabrina went on, although she quickly snatched a few more from the plate, just in case her aunts decided to zap them away. "Or family reunions or decorations."

Hilda scrunched up her face as she thought. "What else is there?"

"I don't know. All I know is that it just doesn't

*feel* like Christmas," Sabrina tried to explain. She toyed with the end of her long, straight, blond hair. "I mean, the great thing about being a witch is that you get to do all kinds of neat things that normal people can't do. But it doesn't seem fair. I mean, what good is being a witch, with all kinds of special powers, if you can't have what normal people have? I just feel so left out."

Her aunts nodded sympathetically.

"Being a witch is a mixed bag," Hilda agreed.

"I wish Mom were here," Sabrina muttered. "She'd know what to do to make it feel like Christmas."

Zelda and Hilda exchanged a pained look over Sabrina's head.

"I've got the perfect idea," Hilda said, jumping up. She snapped her fingers, and suddenly all their winter clothes changed into festive Mexican costumes, with embroidered blouses and flowing skirts. "In Mexico," Hilda recited, "children celebrate Christmas by taking turns at trying to break open a colorful piñata filled with candy."

Sabrina struggled with the blindfold over her eyes as Hilda stuffed a long, thick stick into her hands.

"Come on, Sabrina!" Aunt Zelda shouted, joining in the festivities. "Hit the piñata!"

"I don't know . . ." Sabrina said unenthusiastically.

"Oh, come on, it'll be fun," Hilda said. "I filled it up with lots of goodies."

But Sabrina just pulled off her blindfold and handed the stick to her aunt. "You hit it, Aunt Hilda. I think I just want to go upstairs."

She snapped herself back into her school clothes as she hurried up to her room. Once there she grabbed a framed photo of her mom and flopped down onto her bed on her stomach. She really missed her mom—it was the only thing she didn't like about being a witch. She hadn't even had a chance to talk with her about the changes that had happened to her.

"I don't get it, Sabrina," Salem said, swishing his long, black tail as he lounged on the windowsill of her big bay window. "What's the big deal? Who needs this Santa business, anyway? You're a witch!"

"So?" Sabrina said.

"So?!" Salem exclaimed. He flipped over and leaped onto the quilt-covered bed beside her. "So you can just whip up any present you want with a flick of your finger, or a spell from your book of magic. It's the ultimate in at-home shopping. And the best thing about it? Everything fits and there's never a fee for shipping and handling."

"Yeah, right." Sabrina sat up and set the picture frame on her bedside table. Then her eyes lit up. "Yeah—right! I can!"

What better way to beat the holiday blues than splurging on a major shop-till-you-drop jingle-bell binge?

Sabrina's mind flooded with memories of all the

Christmas presents she'd yearned for, hoped for, begged for over the years—the ones that hadn't shown up under the tree on Christmas morning.

She giggled and shot a conspiratorial glance at Salem. "I shouldn't . . . should I?"

Salem twitched his nose and purred. "Go for it, girl. 'Tis the season to be jolly. And while you're at it, how about whipping up a nice cat-toy for me?"

Sabrina bit her finger, trying to decide what to conjure up first. *Is this too self-indulgent?* she wondered.

Maybe on a regular afternoon. But it was Christmastime, her parents were at opposite ends of the cosmos doing their own thing, and she'd been a good girl all year long.

Well, most of the year, if you didn't count the time she'd turned Libby into a pineapple . . . or the time she'd turned Libby into a paper-eating goat . . . or the time she'd turned Libby into a greasy-haired geek . . . or—

*Never mind!* With a shake of her head, Sabrina shoved those thoughts aside and got down to business.

She rubbed her hands together to warm up her fingers, then pointed at her old rocking chair.

> *"Huggable hunk that I loved from afar,*
> *Now appear in yon rocking chair . . ."*

"Ouch!" Salem cringed, pawing his pointed black ear. "Robert Frost must be spinning in his grave! Your meter's not bad, kid, but how about watching those rhymes?"

"Sorry, I'm in a hurry," Sabrina said with a shrug. "Besides, it's not like I'm turning it in to my English teacher or anything. Who cares, as long as it works."

"It's called style," Salem pointed out dryly.

Sabrina repeated the spell and twirled her pointed finger at her rocking chair.

Zap! The air sparkled with lavender glitter and the tiny bell-like notes of a glockenspiel as the huge, purple teddy bear she'd admired in Milton's Department Store when she was five years old appeared in the rocker. Sabrina squealed in delight and bounced over to give the big bear a hug.

"Oh, brother," Salem groaned. *"That's* your hunk? Give me a break, Sabrina! You can have anything in the universe, and the best you can come up with is a purple teddy bear? Ohhhh, if I weren't trapped in this tedious cat's body . . ."

"All right, all right, I'm not done yet." Sabrina straightened the big satin bow beneath her teddy's chin. "It's just that I wanted this bear so much. . . ."

Sabrina paced the room, trying to think of something else. At last her eyes lit up and she grinned. Of course! Hadn't she written Santa a dozen letters when she was six, asking for a very special present? It was the year her mother had given her that "why Santa doesn't always bring us everything we ask for" lecture. She'd known, deep in her heart, that she wouldn't be getting it. But somehow she'd hoped just the same.

Now she *could* have it!

She pointed at the middle of her room and mumbled some words.

*"Neiiiiigh!"*

"Uh, Sabrina—there's a horse standing in the middle of your bedroom," Salem pointed out nervously. "A rather big one, I might add, with huge, dangerous hooves . . ."

"I know—isn't he great?" She snapped her fingers, adorning herself in the coolest Queen of the Rodeo outfit she could imagine, complete with red cowboy hat, fringed jacket and riding skirt, and red hand-tooled cowboy boots. "Yeee-haw!" she squealed, twirling a lasso—which quickly got tangled in the room's chandelier light fixture. After only about four tries, she was able to pull herself up into the horse's saddle.

"I am definitely not into horses, Sabrina," Salem complained as he pawed at his head, trying to knock off the matching tiny, red cowboy hat she'd given him. "And can we lose the hat, please?"

Sabrina sat down on her bed and slowly pulled off the cowboy hat. The horse was really nice, but as a child she'd only dreamed of a fantasy horse. This one would need her to groom it and exercise it daily, and she'd need to take riding lessons, and there was the cost of feeding and boarding him, too. She wondered if there was a neighborhood rule about keeping horses in the backyard. Hmm, she was beginning to see why her mom had said no that year. A horse was not a toy, but a living creature who needed a lot of care and attention.

With a sigh, she sent Trigger back to his ranch, and settled for a nice framed snapshot of her riding him, which she placed on her shelf.

Over the next half hour she tried filling her room with the coolest clothes, jewelry, CDs, computer equipment, and shoes—*dozens* of shoes. Boxes towered to the ceiling, and shopping bags littered the floor.

Salem purred happily as he pawed through his own pile of packages filled with catnip toys and jeweled collars.

She twirled around in the middle of it all and gushed, "Isn't this so cool, Salem? Aren't I the luckiest girl in the world?"

"Who are you trying to convince?" Salem said dryly. "Me or yourself?"

Sabrina's smile faded. She plopped down on her bed and her shoulders sagged.

With an unexpected snap, she sent it all back.

"Sabrina, wait!" Salem cried as he lunged for his own disappearing pile of presents. "What did you have to go and do that for? Do you know how hard it is for me to dial the phone and use a charge card with these paws?"

Insulted, he leaped from the windowsill and trotted out of the room. "I think I'll go drown my sorrows in a bowl of cream."

Sabrina sat in her window seat and stared out into the gathering darkness.

Moments before, her room had been jammed with fabulous presents. But it didn't help. Inside she still felt empty.

What good were Christmas presents that you gave yourself?

Somehow it just wasn't the same.

☆

# Chapter 4

☆

**S**tocks? Bonds? A new scratching post might be
nice." Salem purred thoughtfully as he stretched
languorously in a patch of sunlight on the Spellman's kitchen floor. "A case of tuna's always good.
Or maybe a couple of those nice toy mice made out
of fuzzy gray felt—the kind stuffed with catnip?
You can *never* have too many of *those.*"

"I didn't ask what *you* want for Christmas,
Salem," Sabrina said with a shake of her head. "I
need ideas for Harvey." It was almost Christmas,
and she still hadn't gotten him a present. She
wanted it to be something majorly special, especially since she was worried that his feelings for her
might be undergoing some kind of renovation.

Guys were definitely harder to buy for than girls,
Sabrina mused. She'd already gotten Jenny this
cool crystal on a silver chain and a book of quotes

44

from famous poets about the value of individuality. But the stuff piled up at the malls in the men's departments was all navy blue or somehow connected to shaving soap or otherwise unimaginative and boring.

"How about a nice abacus," Aunt Zelda suggested as she made one of the ancient counting instruments appear on the kitchen table. She flicked the wooden beads along the rods and smiled at their gentle clicking sound. "I loved the one I had as a child—until *someone* borrowed it and broke it," she added, casting an accusing eye at her younger sister. "An abacus might help Harvey improve his math grade."

Hilda ignored the barb and shook her head. "Nah, that's way too boring." She drummed her fingers on the tabletop, thinking, then clapped her hands. "I've got it! How about a game of zero-g basketball on the moon—with Michael Jordan?"

Sabrina's eyes nearly popped out. "I can do that?"

Zelda rolled her eyes and propped her hand on her hip. "Hilda, are you out of your mind? It's the middle of basketball season! You know it's virtually impossible to get a game going with Mike this time of year."

Hilda's shoulders slumped. "Yeah, I guess you're right. Sorry, Sabrina. Maybe for his birthday."

Sabrina nodded, disappointed. That would have been really special, since Harvey played on the Fighting Scallions basketball team.

As she let her gaze wander around the room, trying to come up with ideas, her eyes fell on an old portrait hanging in an antique frame on the wall. The stern-looking woman in the painting wore her dark hair pulled back into a severe bun, and her prim, black dress was topped with a lace collar fastened at her throat with a cameo pin. *I wonder what Aunt Louisa might suggest,* Sabrina wondered. *Sturdy shoes? A year's supply of castor oil?*

"What about you, Aunt Louisa?" Sabrina asked out loud. "Any ideas?"

"How about a Smashing Pumpkins CD?" Aunt Louisa suggested with a giggle, as only the lips on the portrait moved. "They rock *my* world!"

Sabrina laughed. The first time she'd heard the portrait talk, when she'd first come to live with her aunts, she'd nearly fainted. But since then she'd seen a lot weirder stuff than a painting with moving lips. "Great idea, Aunt Louisa," she told the portrait, "only . . . I think he already has all their CDs."

Zelda had a few more historical suggestions, Hilda had a few more outrageous ideas, and Salem continued to advocate a shopping spree at the mega-pet store at the mall, but none of their ideas seemed right to Sabrina.

"Maybe you should drop in on the young man," Aunt Louisa suggested. "Catch him unawares. See him in his home environment and try to find out what he likes. You know, *spy* a little? Case the joint? *Snoop?* You can find out a lot of useful information," the framed old lady said, "just by hanging around and watching and listening."

*You should know, Aunt Louisa,* Sabrina thought—wishing she could be a picture hanging on the wall in Harvey's house.

"I don't know . . ." Zelda said warily. "You have to be careful sneaking up on people. . . ."

"I say, go for it!" Hilda said.

Did her aunts ever agree? *Only about my bedtime and my allowance,* she reminded herself.

"Well, spying might be going a little too far," Sabrina agreed. "But maybe if I just drop by . . ."

She grabbed her down coat and flew out the door.

Sabrina stood on Harvey's front porch, her hand frozen halfway to the door. And not just because it was so cold outside.

Inside the house, someone was singing. And, amazingly, it sounded a lot like . . . Elvis?

Sabrina cupped her cold hands around her eyes as she peeked through the glass panel beside the door. She could see Harvey alone in his living room. Sabrina smothered a giggle with her hand.

Thinking he was all alone, Harvey was doing this hilarious impersonation of the King of Rock and Roll while lip-synching to a recording of Elvis's "Blue Christmas." *He looks so cute!* Sabrina thought. She could have stood there on the porch just watching him for hours.

Too bad it was way freezing outside.

With a sigh, Sabrina rapped on the glass pane, and Harvey froze, his eyes darting to the door. Sabrina peered through the glass with a huge smile and waved.

But instead of looking happy to see her, Harvey looked panicked. He grabbed up something on the living room couch and stuffed it into a paper grocery bag. What was *that* all about? Then he ran over to his parents' old record player and lifted the needle arm from the revolving record.

Only then did he come to the door. "Hi, Sabrina," he said, grinning now, though his cheeks were flushed with a faint blush.

"Hi, Harvey."

"Uh, how are you?"

"Um, a little cold?"

"Oh, sorry! Come on in!" Harvey held the door open, and Sabrina hurried into the warm living room, rubbing her cold hands together.

"So . . . was that Elvis I heard a minute ago?" Sabrina began.

"Yeah, it's one of my parents' old vinyl records," Harvey explained apologetically. "They have an entire collection of his albums. I know it's old stuff, but I dunno, I really like it."

"It's okay, I like old stuff, too," Sabrina said quickly. "Huh, you should see my *aunts'* record collection. It goes *way* back!" She decided not to mention that they even had recordings of some of Mozart's early concerts. Witches had had the technology long before Edison invented the gramophone. "I think Elvis is really cool, too."

"You do?" Harvey exclaimed in surprise.

"Definitely. He was, like, the first rock and roll star who totally freaked out parents," Sabrina said. "He was a pioneer."

Harvey's smile nearly melted Sabrina's heart. "I knew you'd understand." Then he sighed. "I wish I could sing like him."

"I like the way you sing," Sabrina said. Sometimes he hummed along with the radio in the car, or when they took long walks.

Harvey just blushed. "So, why'd you come over?" he asked. "I mean, of course I'm glad you did. But was there something you wanted?"

Sabrina suddenly had a great idea—a great way to find out what Harvey would like for Christmas. "I have this problem I need your help with."

Harvey's eyes grew worried and he reached for Sabrina's hands. "Sure, anything. Is everything okay?"

"No, nothing like that," Sabrina said quickly. "It's just I'm having trouble finding a Christmas present for my cousin. He's a boy. Like you. Your age. I thought maybe you could go Christmas shopping with me tomorrow and help me find something that he might like."

Harvey glanced at the paper bag in the recliner in the corner, as if pondering something. But then he glanced back at Sabrina and nodded. "Yeah, sure, I can go. But I don't know if I can help or not," he added. "I don't even know your cousin or what he likes."

"That's okay," Sabrina reassured him. "He's a *lot* like you. In fact, he could be your twin brother."

After school the next day Sabrina waited for Harvey by the chorus room door. Harvey was way too shy to have joined the chorus—he was in it by mistake. When he'd gotten his class schedule that year, the school computer had accidentally signed him up for chorus, instead of calculus. He'd tried to explain that the first day of class, but Mr. Beasley was so delighted to see him—so few guys had signed up for chorus—that Harvey couldn't bring himself to explain that it was all a big mistake. Harvey had a hard time saying no to anyone. Even the school computer.

His shyness was one of the things Sabrina really liked about Harvey. She didn't trust guys who came on too loud and aggressive, like salesmen, so sure of their good looks, so positive that they were driving girls wild.

Sabrina looked inside the chorus room. About fifty kids stood on a graduated platform arranged by what voice part they sang—soprano, alto, tenor, or bass. But Sabrina didn't see Harvey anywhere. Had he forgotten their plans?

No—*there* he was. In the back row, hiding behind his sheet music. She'd recognize his hair anywhere.

And two inches away stood Libby Chessler. *What was a soprano doing next to a bass?* Sabrina wanted to know indignantly.

"Libby," Mr. Beasley called out. "Shouldn't you be over here, with the other sopranos?"

Libby made a face that would melt a metal music stand, but she moved to where the music teacher pointed.

The final bell had rung, but the chorus was staying over, rehearsing for their big Christmas Eve concert at the mall. Sabrina hummed along quietly as the chorus ran through the same old carols and Hanukkah songs they sang every year. This year they'd added some songs about Kwanzaa, the African-American festival held in late December.

The chorus sounded nice—but the concert was a little boring. It could be any Christmas concert, anywhere, USA.

*They need something to wake it up,* Sabrina thought. *Something different. Something a little more fun.*

Then she spotted something lying on top of the upright piano in the corner. It was the sheet music for "Blue Christmas." Hmmm . . . After a quick glance around, Sabrina held up her right hand and blew softly across her palm.

A soft current of air swept toward the piano and blew the sheet music off the piano.

Sabrina made sure the air current carried the paper toward Mr. Beasley, who stood before a music stand in front of the chorus. With a little swirl of her finger, the sheet music landed right at the teacher's feet.

"Would somebody please shut that door?" he said as he bent to pick up the music. "There's a draft."

Sabrina closed the door, then quietly slipped into a seat at the back of the room.

Mr. Beasley tucked the sheet music into the stack on his music stand and got ready to go over the next number.

Sabrina made a face. Couldn't he take a hint?

Quickly she tapped her finger to her palm, and a tiny mosquito appeared—which required a good dose of magic in the middle of December. Then she sent it off to buzz around Mr. Beasley's head—but she updated the insect's ordinary buzz to a buzzy insect version of "Blue Christmas."

Mr. Beasley swatted at his ear a few times, then began humming as he looked through his sheet music.

*Yes! It worked!* Sabrina thought, rather proud of her buggy subterfuge.

The music teacher was humming "Blue Christmas."

Suddenly he stopped and looked up at his chorus, who were waiting expectantly, and a smile slowly lit up his face. "I've got it!" he exclaimed. He rustled through the sheet music on his stand till he found the one Sabrina had sent him by air mail. He took it over to Miss Pennyfeather, their accompanist on the piano, then began to scan the crowd of kids.

"I need an Elvis," he said. "Someone from the bass section."

There were only four guys in the Westbridge chorus whose voices had changed permanently enough to sing bass. Walter Curry, a two hundred pound guy who looked half asleep. A couple of guys who looked like science teachers.

And Harvey.

With his cool clothes, thick brown hair, and majorly cool sideburns.

"Harvey Kinkle!" Mr. Beasley called out. "I've got a wonderful idea! *You're* going to sing a solo!"

Harvey peeked out from behind his sheet music. "Me?" he squeaked. "Uh, I don't know . . ."

"Oh, come, come, come, you'll be perfect!" Mr. Beasley exclaimed, shoving through the stands to grab his arm and pull him down front. "You have a fine voice. It will be perfect. It'll be *fun!*"

Harvey looked mortified, and Sabrina began to have misgivings. She wanted to give her favorite shy guy a chance to shine, not humiliate him. Had she made a mistake?

"Uh, Mr. Beasley . . ." Harvey began.

"Run through the first bars, Miss Pennyfeather," Mr. Beasley asked the pianist. "Harvey, do you by any chance know the words to 'Blue Christmas'?"

"Well, as a matter of fact, yes, sir, I do, but—"

"Excellent!" Mr. Beasley exclaimed, clapping his hands. "Let's give it a try."

Sabrina bit her finger. Harvey was trapped in the spotlight by his inability to say no.

*It's okay,* Sabrina told herself. *He sings pretty good. I bet once he gets started, he'll be fine.*

The pianist began at the top. Harvey shuffled his feet and cleared his throat.

"Go ahead, Harvey," Mr. Beasley prompted. "Don't be shy."

Harvey winced and began to sing—so quietly at first, one could hardly hear him. "I'll have a blue Christmas without you . . ." But his shyness made his voice crack. And when he glanced nervously around and spotted Sabrina sitting at the back of the room, he blushed furiously as his voice trailed off.

A few kids snickered.

Sabrina cringed.

Was it true what they said? *You always hurt the one you love . . .*

Harvey was about to totally humiliate himself— and it was all her fault!

# Chapter 5

If only she could turn back the hands of time.

Forget that she'd ever had such a ridiculous idea as making Harvey the center of attention.

But that was one of the things that witches couldn't do.

Well, the Witches' Council had the power under certain *special* circumstances to turn back time. But they only did it under extreme circumstances, and they'd already granted Sabrina one time-reversal request that had allowed her to relive her first day of school at Westbridge High. And that one had not been easy to get.

She had the feeling they wouldn't be so eager to do it again. At least, not to help a mortal in a situation they would consider unimportant to the running of the cosmos.

And besides, the Witches' Council was ten million light-years away, and she'd have to go all the way home even to take the shortcut through the Spellman sisters' upstairs linen closet. There just didn't seem time to ask.

So Sabrina did the first thing that popped into her head.

"Merry Christmas, Harvey," she whispered, then softly chanted a quickly composed magic spell with a slight rock and roll beat:

> *"Uh, with a shake of the hips,*
> *and a lip that curls,*
> *Give Harv the voice of Elvis*
> *so he can wow the girls."*

She wasn't particularly happy with the last part, but when you were in a hurry you had to work with whatever rhymes you could think of.

Sabrina flung her fingertip toward Harvey, and he was instantly showered in what looked like a brief shimmer of sugary, multicolored sparkles.

Mr. Beasley did a double take, but what happened next made him totally forget the unusual splash of glitter.

Harvey began to sing like the King.

His voice came out rich and deep and smooth, without the tiniest stutter. Sabrina realized then that he didn't just sound kind of *like* Elvis.

Elvis's voice was pouring from Harvey's mouth!

Harvey looked astonished by the mellow tones

emanating from his vocal chords. As he began to relax and let the music happen, he even threw in a few Elvisy moves. In fact, he became so wrapped up in the experience of making this astonishing music, he seemed to forget that everyone was staring at him.

Mr. Beasley just stood there with his mouth hanging open.

The other kids in the chorus listened in rapt admiration, then cheered wildly when he finished the number.

Sabrina jumped up, clapping like mad.

Harvey was a big hit!

Suddenly everyone was psyched about the concert, and Mr. Beasley and his students excitedly made plans. And in the middle of it all, Sabrina saw something absolutely wonderful.

She saw Harvey smile.

A magical glow that had nothing to do with witchcraft filled her heart.

When the rehearsal was finally over, and Harvey was finally able to extract himself from all his admirers, he grabbed his backpack and hurried over to where Sabrina sat waiting.

"Hi, Sabrina, thanks for waiting," he said, then asked shyly, "So, uh, what'd you think?"

"Oh, Harvey, you sounded wonderful!" Sabrina gushed. "I had no idea you could sing like that!"

"Neither did I." A puzzled look clouded his expression for a moment as he pondered that thought, then he shrugged it off and smiled. Harvey was an uncomplicated kind of guy who took life as it came, with few questions asked.

"So—ready to go Christmas shopping?" he asked Sabrina as they headed out into the hallway.

But Sabrina just smiled and shook her head. "No need to now. I think I've found the perfect gift."

Sabrina yawned and threw back her covers. Two days till Christmas. Time to put in her yearly request.

Sabrina went to the bookshelf by her window and picked up her snowdome. It was a thick glass globe about the size of a baseball on a polished mahogany base. It had a lot more snow inside than those cheap, plastic, touristy ones you could get that said FLORIDA, with alligators seesawing inside. Actually . . . those were kind of cool, too, she had to admit, in a funky, junky sort of way.

But this one was special.

Her mother had given her this one for Christmas one year when she was still little, and Sabrina had been surprised her mother would trust her with something so fragile. When you gently turned this snowdome upside down, then quickly right side up again, a silent blizzard of white swirled around in the thick clear liquid for a really long time before slowly settling to the ground. Inside was a small log cabin, surrounded by three tall, dark green ever-green trees. The windows were painted a cheery yellow, so they seemed to glow with candlelight. As a child, Sabrina had longed to go inside, to see who might live in such a cozy, happy-looking house.

Every year since her mother gave it to her, she'd used it to wish for a white Christmas. Some years it snowed, some years it didn't, but she liked pretend-ing that, when it did, it was because the snowdome held some special magic to turn the world into a snow-white fairyland.

She'd had no way of knowing then that the magic was in her.

Sabrina curled up on her window seat and tucked her bare feet beneath her long, white nightgown, then gave the snowdome a gentle shake. She closed her eyes and whispered, "I wish it would snow for Christmas. . . ."

"You wouldn't if you had to walk barefoot through it like I do," Salem drawled petulantly as he trotted into the room and leaped onto the window seat beside her.

Sabrina opened her eyes. She hoped his negative comment wouldn't ruin the vibes of her wish. "So we'll get you some little red boots."

Salem cocked his head a moment, thinking. "That could work. . . ."

Sabrina scratched him behind the ears, then glanced out her window. A few clouds dotted the sky, but nothing like the thick clouds that looked like a herd of running sheep that usually forecast snow.

Well, there was still time.

"I wonder if there's a spell for snow," Sabrina wondered aloud.

"There is," Salem replied, grooming his paws. "But *I'll* never tell."

*Oh, well,* she decided as she replaced the snowdome on her shelf. *I think I'd rather just trust the dome.*

That afternoon the chorus was scheduled to make its first appearance at the mall.

"Gee, Sabrina, I don't know if I can go through with this," Harvey was saying as they sat in the mall parking lot in Harvey's car. He looked really cool dressed up in a red cable-knit sweater, black corduroys, and sleek black boots. Fortunately Mr. Beasley only wanted him to *sing* like Elvis. He hadn't insisted on making him wear one of those creepy white sequined jumpsuits from the seventies to try and *look* like Elvis.

"Harvey," Sabrina said confidently, "you'll be fine."

"Yeah?"

"*Yeah.* Piece of cake. I promise." She opened her car door. "Come on, I'll walk you in."

Harvey didn't move.

"Come on!"

"I can't!" Harvey gasped. "My hands . . ."

"What's wrong?"

"They won't let go of the steering wheel!"

Once again Sabrina experienced some doubts about her "Christmas present" to Harvey. But then she remembered how happy he'd looked at the rehearsal when everyone had complimented his singing. So she jumped out and ran around to his side of the car and gently pried his fingers from the steering wheel. "Come on, Harvey," she said gently, and on impulse gave him a quick kiss on the cheek. "I know you can do it."

That seemed to help. "Okay, Sabrina," he said with a lopsided grin as he got out of the car. "I'll do it—for you."

"Thanks, Harvey, that's sweet," Sabrina said. "But do it for yourself. You sounded great the other day. The crowds at the mall are gonna *love* you."

Harvey hunched his shoulders against the cold wind as they hurried to the mall entrance. "Did you have to say *that word?*" he asked her.

"What word?"

"Crowds."

Once inside, Harvey went to warm up with the other kids from the chorus, so Sabrina walked over to nearby Santa Land to see how Jenny's job as an elf was going.

"You look festive," Sabrina teased her friend.

Jenny glanced down at her official elf costume: a green bodysuit, a short green felt skirt—with real

61

little candy canes tied on with green ribbon—plus green gloves, green tights, pointy green elf shoes with bells on the toes, and a floppy green hat. "I used to like green. . . ," she muttered, sadly shaking her head.

Sabrina laughed. "Don't worry, you look great." She glanced around, and realized there was a long line of fidgety kids waiting to sit on Santa's lap. "So where's old Kris Kringle?"

"Search me," Jenny said, rolling her eyes. She lowered her voice so the kids couldn't hear. "This is the worst Santa I've ever seen. He shows up late, and he keeps going on these long breaks where nobody can find him. Plus, his eyes are always bloodshot and his beard looks totally fake; I can't believe any kids even bother to talk to him. I think Mr. Humbert, my boss, would fire him if he could."

"So how come he doesn't?" Sabrina asked. "He sounds like a real creep."

"He can't," Jenny said. "Do you know how hard it is to find somebody to play Santa two days before Christmas?"

Jenny had a point. Too bad for the kids, though. Sabrina had never really liked mall-Santas when she was growing up—they'd scared her, and she'd usually refused to sit on their laps. But there'd been one once, at a Christmas party her parents had thrown. He had been so sweet and jolly—with a real white beard that he insisted she pull—that Sabrina had been convinced he was the *real* Santa.

Of course, she realized now that he'd just been some sweet old man.

Soon they heard piano music, and although they could see the stage from Santa Land, Sabrina told her friend good-bye so she could get closer and maybe give Harvey some moral support.

The mall was pretty busy, but as the chorus began with a pleasant version of "It's Beginning to Look a Lot Like Christmas," most shoppers only glanced curiously at the stage before hurrying off to fill their arms with more packages. A couple of old ladies came over and sat down in the metal folding chairs near the front. And Sabrina noticed a young couple stop and park their stroller so their curly-haired toddler could hear "Jingle Bells." She also noticed a few of the students' parents who had come to videotape their kids singing at the mall. But that was about it.

Not exactly a sellout crowd.

As usual, Harvey stood in the back row, hiding behind his sheet music. But unlike usual, Sabrina could hear, if she listened closely, the rich tones of Elvis filling out the bass section. She crossed her fingers and waited for Harvey's solo.

After a couple of numbers Libby stepped up to the mike to make a plug for the school's Wish Tree, which was located near Santa Land. "I'm sure we can all find time in our busy schedules to pick up some little something for an unfortunate child," Libby said. "It takes only a few minutes, and it can really make you feel better."

*Ick,* Sabrina thought. *Leave it to Libby to make giving to charity sound like getting your annual flu shot.*

"And be sure to stop by Bill and Bobbie's Newsstand," she added, "for a copy of the December issue of *Beautiful Living New England,* which includes an insightful story on one of Westbridge's leading families. Only four ninety-five a copy and truly worth the—"

"Thank you, Libby," Mr. Beasley interrupted as he took over the mike. "And now, we have a special treat for you. . . ."

*Uh-oh, here it comes.* Sabrina crossed her fingers as Harvey reluctantly made his way to the front. Libby grabbed him on the way and whispered something in his ear.

Sabrina didn't know what she said, but she didn't like that it made him smile and whisper something back.

As he came to the front, Mr. Beasley smiled at him and signaled for Mrs. Pennyfeather to begin playing.

The intro began and Harvey gulped, clutching the microphone in his hands.

When it came time for him to start, he opened his mouth and nothing came out.

The pianist glanced at Mr. Beasley, then began the intro one more time.

*Oh, Harvey!* Sabrina wiggled her finger at him and whispered a chant:

"When singing on stage makes you squirm
 with distress,
Just look at my face and see none of the
 rest."

Sabrina could see when the *zing!* reached Harvey, because his eyes flew open and he shivered slightly before relaxing into a lopsided grin not unlike those that Elvis used to wear onstage. And this time, when it was time for him to sing the opening lines of the song, he opened his mouth and Elvis's rich voice rang out.

And then Sabrina noticed something funny happening.

Shoppers stopped yacking and turned toward the stage, their mouths hanging open in wonder. A crowd began to gather. A gang of middle school girls dashed out of nearby Mad Mike's Music and Video and clustered at the front of the stage.

Sabrina noticed that a few women, who looked like they might have been teenagers in the fifties, actually had these really dreamy looks on their faces as they swayed to the slow ballad.

And when Harvey finished with those last mournful lines about being sad and lonely on Christmas, the large crowd erupted in applause. A few of the middle school girls up front even squealed.

"All right, Harvey!" Sabrina said as she joined in the applause. She waved at him, but he couldn't seem to see her in the crowd.

The chorus sang another song, but the crowd

asked for more Elvis, so Mr. Beasley thrust a microphone in Harvey's hand and got him to sing lead on the rest of the songs.

Sabrina was so proud of Harvey.

But when the concert was over, she couldn't get close enough to tell him so.

Her "perfect" Christmas present had backfired.

Harvey was surrounded by a huge crowd of adoring girls!

# Chapter 6

Uh-oh—this is definitely not a good sign." Hilda elbowed her sister in the ribs as they stood in Sabrina's doorway.

"What do you mean?" Sabrina muttered. "I'm reading Christmas stories to Salem. What better way to get in the Christmas spirit?"

Zelda plucked the book from her niece's hand—a well-worn copy of *How the Grinch Stole Christmas.* "I *don't* think you're supposed to cheer when the Grinch steals the tree!"

"Hey, wait," Salem protested. "She was just getting to the good part—the part about the roast *beast.*"

"Never mind," Zelda said as she tucked the book back onto Sabrina's shelf.

Then she and Hilda stood side by side, staring

down their noses at her with seriously expectant looks on their faces.

*Uh-oh,* Sabrina thought. One half-mortal half-witch teenager didn't stand a chance against the two Spellman women when they ganged up on her. She wondered how her father had managed to grow up with these two and still be in one piece.

"Uh, don't you guys have something to go off and argue about?" Sabrina suggested lamely.

"Sabrina . . ." Aunt Zelda said, a warning note in her voice. "Won't you tell us what's bothering you?"

Sabrina wanted to, but her aunts had often warned her about meddling in the lives of mortals. They had a saying in the supernatural realm, that *"terrrrrrible* things" could happen when you tried to manipulate people's lives.

She should have known better than to try to make Harvey happy with tricks of witchcraft.

And the worst part? He *did* seem happy—while she was stuck with the miserable consequences.

Harvey was suddenly so popular that he'd developed a permanent new appendage—groupies. And Mr. Beasley had called extra rehearsals to work up some more Elvis numbers before their remaining mall concert on Christmas Eve. He was even adding some doo-wop backup girls to add some fifties style to some of the songs. And one of those backup girls just *had* to be Libby.

So now . . . her dad was too sick to spend Christmas with her.

Her best friend was too busy working at the mall and planning for a holiday family reunion to spend Christmas with her.

And Harvey was too busy being Elvis to hang out with her.

It wasn't fair. If it weren't for Sabrina, they'd be laughing Harvey off the stage, not forming "Harvey the *New* Elvis" fan clubs.

Of course, it was ridiculous to be mad at Harvey, since he had no idea what role Sabrina had played in his new success.

But that didn't keep her from being mad at being ignored!

*Crash!*

A bolt of lightning flashed through the dark thunderclouds that had developed over Sabrina's head.

"Oh, my goodness!" Zelda exclaimed. "This *is* serious—those are cumulonimbus clouds!"

"Well, do something quick!" Salem howled. "Before she starts raining cats and"—he shuddered—*dogs!*"

Zelda laid a smooth, cool hand on Sabrina's brow and *tsk-tsked*. A moment later a two-foot-long thermometer popped into Sabrina's mouth.

"Hey!" she mumbled around the huge glass stick, afraid to move. "Wha's dis for?"

Her aunts ignored her as Hilda grabbed Sabrina's wrist and stared at her own watch. She waited sixty seconds and then—

*Ping!* The thermometer rang like a kitchen timer.

Zelda removed it from Sabrina's mouth and read it. "A-ha. Just as I thought."

"Have I got a fever?" Sabrina asked, worried. "Am I sick? What's it say?"

Hilda peered over her sister's shoulder and read: "You have a bad case of feeling sorry for yourself, compounded by the holiday blues, resulting in an unflattering outbreak of crabbiness."

"Hey, what kind of thermometer is that?" Sabrina grumbled.

"You need to see a doctor," Hilda said.

"A witch doctor," Zelda added with a firm nod.

"Witch doctor?" Sabrina exclaimed. "You mean, like, we have to go to Africa?"

Her aunts laughed and shook their heads.

"Not *that* kind of witch doctor," Hilda said.

They snapped their fingers overhead and said together, *"This* kind of witch doctor!"

Instantly Sabrina found herself sitting in a very ugly, very uncomfortable orange plastic chair in a doctor's waiting room whose walls were the color of dead celery.

In other words, it looked just like a regular doctor's office—except for the knee-deep, swirly, pink, misty stuff floating along the floor.

And the gnome working the receptionist desk.

"The doctor will see you now," the gnome announced. As Sabrina and her aunts went through the door, she noticed a sign that said Dr. Fixit, Witch Doctor and Supernatural Surgeon.

"I should warn you," Zelda whispered. "Dr.

Fixit is *very* good, but a bit . . . odd. Try not to let his mannerisms bother you."

Dr. Fixit invited Sabrina to sit on his examining table, which actually looked like a table from the school cafeteria.

He circled her with a glowing, humming iron bar that blipped every few seconds. "Mmm-hmmm. Mmm-hmmm. Umm-*hmmm!*" He rubbed his chin, then rushed to his desk and scribbled something on a small white prescription pad, which he then ripped off with a flourish and stuffed into Sabrina's hand. "Next!" he shouted as he hustled the three Spellman women out of the office.

Out in the waiting room Sabrina frowned at the slip of paper, then turned it upside down. "I can't read his handwriting," she complained. "It just looks like a bunch of doodly palm trees. What does it say?"

Zelda took it and slipped on her reading glasses. "Hmmm, let's see. Ahhh. Excellent!"

Hilda snatched it from her sister's hand and read. "Whoopee!" she squealed.

"What? *What?*" Sabrina begged.

" 'You're suffering from a bad case of feeling sorry for yourself, compounded by the holiday blues, resulting in an unflattering outbreak of crabbiness,' " Hilda read, "which we—"

"Already knew," Sabrina chimed in. "So what's the cure?"

"Dr. Fixit says that, instead of Christmas trees, you need *palm* trees," Zelda explained.

"And his prescription?" Hilda announced, all smiles and dimples. "Hawaii and Happy Drops!"

The flight to Honolulu on the island of Oahu was quick and uneventful. Normally, a flight by airplane from New England would have taken about ten hours, with a one-hour layover in L.A., with the risks of turbulent weather, bad food, and airport delays.

But Sabrina and her aunts made it in approximately seventeen and two-thirds seconds—via the upstairs linen closet.

Soon she and her aunts were basking in the warm sunshine on the golden beach in front of their pink hotel, surrounded by palm trees swaying in the mild tropical breeze. Aunt Zelda had sensibly donned a stylish wide-brimmed hat and very Hollywood dark sunglasses and slathered on an SPF 45 sunscreen before settling back to read her *Quantum Physics Bimonthly.*

Hilda, on the other hand, was drenched in suntan oil and holding a tanning reflector around her face.

"You'll be sorry in another two hundred years when your skin is prematurely wrinkled from sun damage," Zelda scolded as she turned a page.

"Aw, who cares? I say, live for today," Hilda replied. "You're only young once!"

Sabrina closed her eyes and sighed as she sank back into her lounge chair. Everything was just perfect. Faint Hawaiian music floated on the light breeze. They had a gorgeous view of Diamond Head in the distance. She was wearing a terrific new bikini that Hilda had whipped up for her, in a shade that exactly matched the color of Sabrina's eyes.

Even Libby would be envious.

Hilda twirled a coral-tipped finger as if she were stirring ice cubes in a drink, and a tiny bell tinkled.

Instantly a tall, tanned waiter wearing nothing but Hawaiian-print swim trunks and a lei of fragrant gardenias appeared at their side. With a flash of white teeth, he bent at the waist and served each of the ladies a slushy pink drink. "Papaya-mango-watermelon slushees," he said smoothly. "On the house."

Zelda smiled at the waiter as she took her drink and murmured, "I like the way you order, little sis."

"Thanks, big sis." Hilda dimpled as she accepted her beverage from the young man and added, "What good is a vacation unless you pamper yourself with perfection?" She blew the waiter a kiss as he sauntered off.

*Perfect, everything's just perfect,* Sabrina repeated as she sipped her frozen pink drink. Her eyes drifted closed as she absorbed the experience. Perfect sun, perfect sand, perfect scenery, perfect suntans, and perfect . . .

*Snow.*

For some reason she thought of her snowdome sitting on her shelf back home, and the snug little snow-covered log cabin inside.

Sabrina couldn't believe it. Here she was on the vacation of a lifetime in a Hawaiian paradise, and all she could think of was, *Where's the snow?*

Hawaii was cool, for sure, and she'd absolutely *love* to come back—maybe in a couple of months, like for spring break?

But it *definitely* didn't feel like Christmas.

Christmas was snow and woolly mittens, evergreens and hot chocolate, colored lights and surprises and wishing for the unexpected.

And cold. For Sabrina at least, it definitely had to be cold.

Sweating in a teeny bikini just didn't feel like Christmas.

Lost in thought, she imagined Harvey back home, shuffling along a snowy street with his blue down jacket bunched up to his chin, his cheeks rosy from a brisk wind, humming some corny Christmas carol, snowflakes in his hair . . .

*And probably surrounded by his new fan club of snowbunnies,* Sabrina thought with a frown.

"So, what do you think, Sabrina?" Hilda asked, interrupting her thoughts. "Does this beat the winter blues or *what?*"

"Or what," Sabrina replied with a pout.

*"What?!"*

Sabrina sighed. "I'm sorry, Aunt Hilda and Aunt

Zelda. It's totally wonderful here and everything—
and I really hope we can come back soon, but—"

"You miss Harvey," her aunts said at the same
time.

Sabrina shrugged sheepishly. "How'd you
guess?"

"It's written all over your face," Zelda said with
a sympathetic smile.

*And* the sky," Hilda added, pointing.

Sabrina glanced up and gasped. The one wisp of
a white cloud in the otherwise brilliant blue sky
now spelled out in twenty-foot cursive letters:

# *Harvey*

Sabrina shrieked. "Oh, my gosh—did *I* do that?"
Blushing, she waved her hand in the air as if erasing
a blackboard, and scattered the wisps of cloud to
the far corners of the sky.

Her aunts had warned her you had to be careful
about daydreaming when you were a witch!

"Oh, don't worry, Sabrina," Aunt Zelda said.
"Nobody here knows you or Harvey."

"Hey, I could make our waiter look like Harvey,"
Hilda suggested enthusiastically. "Would that
help?"

Sabrina thought a minute, then shook her head.
She definitely liked the way Harvey looked, but it
wasn't his looks that were important. It was that

special way he was *inside* that she really missed. "Nah, thanks, anyway." She reached toward the bowl of tiny silver-wrapped treats Dr. Fixit had prescribed and popped one in her mouth. "At least these Happy Drops help a little," Sabrina admitted. "What are these things, anyway?"

"Chocolate," Hilda confided.

Sabrina laughed—she should have known. Why else would they call them Happy Drops?

By suppertime the Spellman women were all ready to fly home. Even with the hotel's free hula lessons, Zelda was getting bored intellectually. Sabrina was majorly homesick. And Hilda had managed to acquire a seriously sunburned nose.

"Just my luck," Hilda grumbled as they made their way out of the linen closet back home. "I fly to Hawaii to get a midwinter tan like a jet-setter, and wind up looking like Rudolph the Red-nosed Reindeer!"

Sabrina hurried across the hall to her room and caught Salem lying on her bed, drinking eggnog and sniffling over the final scene of *It's a Wonderful Life*.

"I-I'm not crying," he insisted, tucking his head beneath his paws. "I've just got a piece of lint in my eye."

"Come on, Salem, cheer up," Sabrina said. "I brought you something." She set a tiny plastic hula girl in front of his nose. The black cat swatted it with his paw, and the little figurine shook her grass skirt and plunked her ukelele.

"When I asked you to bring me back a hula girl," Salem drawled, "this isn't exactly what I had in mind."

Sabrina scratched the sour puss behind the ears. "Sorry, Salem, it was the best I could do." She tossed her purse onto her desk, then plopped onto her bed, propping herself up against the antique wooden headboard. "Um, any calls?" she asked, trying to sound nonchalant.

Salem twitched his whiskers. "Nope."

Sabrina's shoulders slumped.

"Oh, wait! There was one—"

"Really?" Sabrina leaned forward. "Who?"

"Let's see," Salem said, swishing his tale. "What was his name. . . ."

"Salem . . ."

"Could it have been . . . Harry?" he said. "No, that doesn't sound right. Harvey? Do you know anybody named Harvey?"

"Oh, you!" Sabrina cried, scooping him into her arms. "I ought to tickle you till you scream."

"Didn't you know? We cats *aren't* ticklish."

"Oh, yeah?" Sabrina tickled him anyway till she found the one tiny spot right under his tummy that made him beg for mercy. "What did he say? Did he leave a message?"

"I'll tell you—*ha, ha, ha!*—if you put me *down!*" Salem shrieked.

77

"Deal." Sabrina laid him down on her bed, where he lay gasping for breath.

"You've got to promise me you won't tell anybody that you managed to tickle a cat," Salem begged. "It's a closely guarded feline secret. If word gets out I squealed, I'll be in big trouble with all the other cats."

"Don't worry," Sabrina teased. "I'll just save it for when I need to torture you. Now, what was Harvey's message?"

Salem repositioned himself into his normal, regal pose, then replied, "He said he missed you and he was sorry he was so busy, but he'll look for you after the Christmas Eve concert at the mall tomorrow night."

*Oh, pooh,* Sabrina thought, flopping back on her pillows. She'd been hoping they could spend all of Christmas Eve together.

Tomorrow night would have to do.

# Chapter 7

Christmas Eve, Sabrina's favorite day of the year.

She'd always loved it better than Christmas Day, because it was still filled with promises and hidden surprises.

Too bad she'd spent most of it playing Scrabble with Salem Saberhagen, would-be emperor of the world. He was a rotten speller, and on top of that, he cheated. Whenever she accused him of making up a word, he always claimed the word was well known—at least to other cats.

But soon she'd be spending Christmas Eve with Harvey. She'd asked her aunts if they wanted to come along and hear the concert; they'd told her thanks, but to run along without them, because they had some things to do.

Sabrina grinned. She loved secrets—although at

her aunts' house, you never knew quite what you'd wind up with.

She rubbed her freezing hands together as she hurried to the entrance to the mall. Maybe she could get some gloves while she was here.

Once inside, Sabrina was overwhelmed. The mall was totally mobbed! From the Dickens Den to Mad Mike's Music and Video to the Too Chic Boutique, frantic last-minute shoppers shoved in and out of the jammed stores.

*They don't look very merry,* Sabrina thought as she made her way through the harried-looking crowd.

As she neared the stage where the chorus was to perform, Sabrina spotted a camera crew and a stylishly dressed man smoothing back his already perfectly styled thick, blond hair.

*I know that face,* Sabrina realized—*and that hair.* It was Hunter Chase, Channel 5's "Seen on the Scene" newsguy.

He must be covering the concert and Wish Tree story for the local news, Sabrina thought.

Cool! Maybe Harvey would be on TV! He'd probably hate it, though, Sabrina thought. But then again, maybe, if he saw how cool he looked and sounded on TV, it would boost his confidence a little.

Sabrina tried to push her way up to the stage, but instead found herself jumping up and down trying to see over a lot of very tall people

*Must be having a basketball sale at the Sports*

*Palace,* she grumbled. *Either that or it's a joint Michael Jordan/Larry Bird family reunion. Why do tall people always push their way to the front of crowds,* she wondered, *when they can see over anybody?* She definitely needed to have a talk with her aunts about the possibility of using witchcraft to add a few inches to her height.

She glanced around. Once she was sure no one was paying any attention, she flicked her pointed fingers at her feet.

Her flat black boots instantly grew some three-inch stacked heels. But it still wasn't enough. She still couldn't see.

Sabrina wondered if word had gotten around about the last concert. When Libby stepped up to the microphone to get things rolling, the crowd surged forward.

This would not do.

She *had* to see Harvey perform.

So she whispered under her breath:

> *"Fat and skinny, short and tall,*
> *Dash away, dash away, dash away, all!"*

Instantly the people in front of her lunged to one side as the crowd parted and an aisle just big enough for Sabrina to squeeze through opened up to the front row.

*Hey,* she rationalized, *it's for Harvey. He deserves to see a familiar face in the front row to help him keep from getting nervous.*

Unfortunately, she also got a front-row seat to Libby's annoying display of fake charity.

"Attention, everybody, and Merry Christmas!" the cheerleader said into the mike, flashing a dazzling smile at Hunter Chase and his "Seen on the Scene" cameraman. "Welcome to Westbridge High School's annual Christmas Concert at the Mall."

There was a smattering of applause, and Libby beamed, bowing as if they were applauding her. Most of the chorus was dressed in either a red or green sweater, with black pants or skirts. But Libby and the rest of the Fighting Scallion cheerleaders had worn their green-and-white cheerleading uniforms.

*Uh-oh,* Sabrina thought. *Bad sign.*

"This year, in conjunction with the concert by the Westbridge High Chorus, the Westbridge High Cheerleaders have devoted many long hours to charity. Our Wish Tree is located next to Santa Land, with the theme 'Feel the Glow.' We cheerleaders encourage you all to"—she made quote marks in the air with her fingers—" 'Feel the Glow' by reaching deep into your hearts—and your wallets—to buy a toy for a poor, underprivileged child. Just think how good it will make you and your family feel on Christmas Eve to know that you've shared a tiny piece of your perfect holiday with a less fortunate child."

Sabrina squirmed. Libby was turning the children's charity into a selfish activity. Give to the

Wish Tree to make yourself feel good? How about to make the *kids* feel good?

"And now," Libby went on, "before the Westbridge High School Chorus Christmas Concert begins, we have a special treat for you." She grinned smugly and waved her fellow cheerleaders onto the stage. "The Westbridge High School Cheerleaders want to give *you* a little Christmas Cheer!"

The girls lined up in their green-and-white uniforms and began to shake their green-and-white pompoms, with Libby in the middle.

> "Shake it to the left,
> Shake it to the right,
> Stand up, sit down,
> Silent Night!"

Sabrina groaned. Libby was turning this whole thing into one big PR event—for Libby Chessler. And the cheer didn't even make any sense.

". . . Go, team!" the cheerleaders finally finished. "Yay, Fighting Scallions!"

The audience applauded politely. Libby continued to jump up and down, shaking her green-and-white pompoms and bowing until Mr. Beasley had to usher her off the stage. "Thank you very much, Libby. Let's give all our cheerleaders a big hand for their wonderful charity work this holiday season."

After the brief applause, Mr. Beasley smiled. "And

now, the Westbridge High Chorus would like to provide you with a little seasonal music to add some cheer to your holiday, and as a special treat—"

A girl in the front row squealed.

Mr. Beasley laughed. "If you stick around for the whole show, we promise you a *very special* solo."

Mr. Beasley glanced back at the chorus, who were all lined up and patiently waiting to perform. He frowned a moment, then smiled as he spotted Harvey hiding in the back row.

The chorus began again with "It's Beginning to Look a Lot Like Christmas" and went on through the traditional favorites, like "Deck the Halls" and "Joy to the World."

Sabrina glanced at Hunter Chase and his Channel 5 "Seen on the Scene" newsteam to see if they were taping. They were, but they all looked pretty bored.

*Hey,* she wanted to holler at them. *Listen up! This is nice music!* She realized she was really enjoying the traditional music.

Then came time for Harvey's solo. Sabrina smiled as she looked for him, but her heart sank when she saw his face. Despite his success from the last concert, he looked as if he was definitely suffering from a major case of stage fright. And it was all her fault. He wouldn't even be here, singing in the concert, if it weren't for her.

She waved to him and he caught her eye. Had the spell from the last concert held? Or was he just glad to see her in the audience? She couldn't tell, but now he grinned and strolled onstage holding a microphone. A blue spotlight encircled him as he began to sing "Blue Christmas."

A few girls squealed. Hunter Chase perked up. She guessed a teenage Elvis impersonator was more colorful than a simple high school chorus concert.

When Harvey finished and took a bow, the audience went wild!

"More! More!" she heard some girls behind her shout.

Mr. Beasley whispered in Harvey's ear, and he grinned a lopsided grin. With an Elvisy shake of his hips, he leaped into a rocking version of "Rockin' Around the Christmas Tree," followed by "Jingle Bell Rock," followed by "Rudolph the Red-Nosed Reindeer."

It was probably the first time Elvis had ever sung "Dreidel, Dreidel, Dreidel." But it was definitely a hit.

At last the chorus sang its closing song, "Silent Night"—with Harvey singing lead vocal in his black-velvet Elvis voice.

When they finished, the crowd exploded in applause. Mr. Beasley beamed, and Harvey gave a shy bow.

Even Libby was grinning as she watched some of the people in the audience head for the Wish Tree to drop in donations of money and toys. The whole concert/Wish Tree project was a huge success.

Then Mr. Humbert, manager of the mall, stepped up to the mike. "Westbridge Mall thanks Westbridge High School for a wonderful concert. In fact," he added, "we'd like to ask you kids to perform again at five. Will you?"

Mr. Beasley turned to his singers. "Okay with you kids?" Most nodded enthusiastically, and so Mr. Beasley turned back and smiled. "We'd *love* to!"

"Great!" Mr. Humbert exclaimed, smiling not at Mr. Beasley or any of the singers but into the Channel 5 news camera. "So all you last-minute shoppers come on out to hear this great group— and remember, we're open till seven for all your holiday gift and entertainment needs."

Sabrina tried to push through the crowd toward Harvey. This was great! Maybe they could get something to eat at the food court before the last concert. "Harvey!" she called. "Over here!"

But Harvey couldn't hear her. Or at least he didn't seem to.

He was too busy being adored by a huge crowd of girls!

☆

# Chapter 8

☆

I've created a monster," Sabrina muttered as she wandered over to Santa Land, where a frazzled-looking Jenny had just put up a sign that read:

**SANTA IS FEEDING HIS REINDEER
BACK IN TEN MINUTES**

"Hey, Pixie," Sabrina said glumly. "Can you take a break and go get something to eat?"

"I guess I better not," Jenny said. "You-know-who just took off, and I have to keep an eye on the throne. Somebody stole one of the plastic poinsettias last night, can you believe it? Hey, how was the concert? It sounded pretty good from over here—at least, what I could hear over the whines and cries of selfish, infantile greed."

"It was great," Sabrina said. "So great, in fact, that we may never see Harvey again. I believe he's leaving after the show for a career in Las Vegas. I hear they love fake Elvises in the casino lounges out there."

Jenny shook her head, causing the little jingle bell on the tip of her elf hat to ring. "He *does* sound like Elvis, though, you've got to admit. Who'd have thought our quiet, shy little Harvey was hiding so much talent?"

"Yeah, who knew?" Sabrina muttered.

Jenny winced and pulled off one of her green shoes. Its pointed toe curved around like something out of a fairy tale, with more jingle bells on the end. "My feet are killing me," she moaned. "These weird shoes are about a half-size too small, and I've been on my feet since noon. The money's pretty good, but I sure wish I could be home with my family. Almost everybody should be there by now. Even my great-grand-mother."

Sabrina sighed. She glanced back at the mob scene near the chorus. No way was she going to get near Harvey any time soon. In fact, he'd probably forgotten all about their plans to meet after the show. She might as well wait around for the mall to close after the second performance.

She had no shopping to do. No parties to go to.

Then she glanced at Jenny. She'd already exchanged presents with her. But she suddenly thought of something that Jenny would love even more. Something that no one else could give her right now.

"Okay, Pixie," Sabrina said firmly, "hand over the hat."

"Huh?"

"And the weird shoes, and that goofy little skirt, and the green tights."

"Sabrina," Jenny said slowly, shaking her head of long, reddish curls in disbelief, "what are you talking about?"

Sabrina grabbed the hat and tugged it on her head. "I'm going to find out what it's like to be in your shoes—literally. You're going home to be with your family, and I'm going to totally humiliate myself by dressing up as Pixie the Elf."

"B-but, Sabrina—!" Jenny's eyes shone with disbelief. "You—you can't! It wouldn't be fair. Oh, I—I couldn't possibly let you—"

"Yes, you can and you will. I have nothing else to do except wait around for Harvey to finish the last concert. And besides, you can't say no, because it's a present. So, Merry Christmas."

Jenny's delighted smile was the best thank-you Sabrina could imagine. "In that case, I accept." Jenny gave Sabrina a quick hug. "You'll make a great elf, and I'm sure Mr. Humbert won't mind, as long as the job is covered. He's had two regular girls out sick with the flu this week, and he's had trouble getting substitutes. Oh, Sabrina, you're the greatest. How can I ever thank you?"

"Just give me a couple of days, I'll think of something," Sabrina teased. Then she grabbed her friend by the arm and began to drag her to the nearest ladies' room. "Now come on, Santa will be back from his break soon, and I've got to change."

Ten quick minutes later, Sabrina waved as her friend headed for the mall exit. Despite the skimpy costume, Sabrina felt all warm inside. Jenny was a special friend, and she deserved a wonderful Christmas Eve.

Besides, Sabrina had never been an elf before. *It might be a lot of fun,* she thought as she headed toward Santa Land.

*Jing-jingle. Jing-jingle.*

*They sure put enough bells on this outfit,* Sabrina thought. *But, hey, I kind of like the short green skirt.* She untied one of the candy canes, unwrapped it, and stuck it in her mouth. *Mmm, Christmas Eve dinner.*

She stopped at the big red-velvet Santa Throne that sat next to the sleigh full of toys pulled by two fake reindeer. The ground was covered with thick pads of glittery cotton to look like snow.

A group of kids in worn clothes lined up impatiently behind the red velvet rope cordoning off the entrance. A tired-looking woman in a worn red coat tried to keep the kids under control.

*Where's Santa?* Sabrina fretted, looking around the busy mall. Where does a guy in a red Santa suit take his break? He couldn't just stroll over to the food court and scarf down a couple of fast-food burgers—it would ruin the magic. There must be an employee break room somewhere, she decided, and wished she'd asked Jenny where it was. She glanced at her watch. The guy had been gone a long time, a lot longer than fifteen minutes. She had an awful feeling in the pit of her stomach.

She hurried over to the crowd of kids and smiled her best elf-smile. "Hi, kids. I'm Pixie!" she said in a chirpy voice.

"We want Santa!" a boy in an old blue parka whined.

"Shhh, Dylan, that's not nice," said the woman in the worn red coat.

"Well, Santa will be back real soon," Sabrina said cheerfully. "I promise!"

"That's what that other elf said," Dylan complained. "And now she's gone, too."

"Well . . . I'm her sister," Sabrina blurted out. "We like to take turns."

"You don't look like sisters," Dylan challenged.

The woman in the worn red coat laid a gentle hand on Sabrina's arm. "Hi, I'm Jane Simmons. Please excuse the kids, honey," she said apologetically. "We're from the Westbridge Children's Home, and I'm afraid the children are a little tired. Our old bus had a flat tire on the way over, and the kids have been waiting all day to see Santa. We're supposed to come and let the children get presents from the Wish Tree at five." She looked at her own watch. "Are we early?" she asked.

"Not exactly," Sabrina said. "Santa seems to be running a little late."

"Where is he?" a big kid at the back jeered. "In the bathroom?" A couple of kids laughed.

Sabrina pointed at the sign. "He's out feeding his reindeer."

"Yeah, right," the boy said.

"There *are* no reindeer," the boy named Dylan said loudly. "Because there is no Sa—"

Sabrina grabbed a red lollipop from a basket next to her station and thrust it at the loud-mouthed boy. "Quiet, kid," she mumbled. "Don't spoil the show."

The boy glared at her, but unwrapped the sucker and stuffed it in his mouth.

"Can I have one?" the little girl beside him asked softly, her eyes big and round.

"Me, too!"

All the kids began jumping up and down, begging for lollipops.

"Sure," Sabrina said brightly as she reached for the red and green basket next to Santa's throne and glanced nervously around. *Santa, where are you? I need you. . . .*

But the only person she saw rushing toward Santa Land was Hunter Chase with a microphone in his hand. His camera crew was not far behind.

"Hi, I'm Hunter Chase, Channel 5's 'Seen on the Scene' newsguy," he said with a fake smile, glancing around. "We're looking for a touching Christmas Eve moment for a live soft-news spot on our five o'clock news. I heard there were gonna be a bunch of orphans—*Ow!*"

Sabrina responded without thinking—she kicked him in the shin with her pointy elf shoes. It was a lot quicker than magic at shutting him up. Then she took his arm and whispered, "Don't call them orphans, okay? They'll hear you."

The newsman frowned as he rubbed his shin. "Sorry. But that's what they are, isn't it? Orphans?"

Sabrina hated the way Hunter made the word sound like a put-down. It wasn't like it was the kids' fault they didn't have moms or dads to bring them to the mall. "They're just kids," she replied. "Nice kids who happen not to have parents, okay?"

Hunter shrugged. "Whatever you say, honey. We just want to shoot them getting their Wish Tree presents so all our viewers can get a nice lump in their throats for Christmas Eve." He glanced around with a bored-looking yawn. "So, where's the guy who's playing Santa?"

"Shhh!" Sabrina said, hoping the children hadn't heard. "He's on a break."

"Yeah, right." Hunter snickered. "Probably a bar break. Any idea when Santa-baby will be back, Trixie?"

Sabrina fumed, but tried to hold on to her polite smile. "I'm sure he'll be back any minute now—and the name's Pixie!"

"Whatever. But can you do anything to move it along? I've got a newsanchor checking in with me for a live report in eight minutes."

Just then Mr. Humbert hurried over, smiling at the newsman and reaching out to shake his hand. "Hey, Hunter, good to see you again. Merry Christmas. Say, did you get those discount coupons I sent over to your office?"

"Sure did. Thanks, Dave."

"Great—super!" Then he turned to Sabrina and his smile instantly disappeared. "Where's Thompkins!" he hissed.

"Who?"

"The guy playing Santa!" Mr. Humbert exclaimed. "Where is he?"

"He went on break," Sabrina explained, "but he never came back."

Mr. Humbert ran a hand through his thinning hair and glanced around at the noisy kids waiting impatiently in line. "I had a bad feeling about that Thompkins guy from the get-go. But what're you gonna do? Fat, unemployed guys without a criminal record are hard to come by this time of year." He glanced nervously around. "Maybe I should check in the employee break room. . . ."

"Hmmm, I sense a great story developing here," Hunter said with a slow grin, butting in and following the mall manager's gaze. "Orphans left crying at the mall when Santa skips town!" He turned to his cameraman to give instructions on how he wanted the story shot. "Hurry, get a shot of that crying kid."

"Oh, terrific," Mr. Humbert muttered sarcastically. "Thanks a lot, pal." Then he turned to Sabrina. "Listen, Pixie, why don't you—hey, who are you?" he demanded suspiciously. "You're not the regular girl."

"Uh, yeah, I know," Sabrina said nervously. "My friend was working the last shift for the regular girl, who's out sick. But then she . . . got sick! Would you believe? Drank some bad eggnog and had to go home. So—lucky for you—I'm filling in for her till the mall closes."

"Yeah, well, whatever." Mr. Humbert rubbed both hands over his sweaty face, then barked, "I've got to get back to that chorus thing. And I've got a problem with a busted security system at the Gap. That cheerleader person arranged to have the Wish Tree presents for the orphanage put over there in Santa's sleigh, so they wouldn't get mixed up with the other donations. She's busy with the concert, and it looks like Santa decided to knock off early for Christmas Eve. So *you* get over there and hand out the presents."

"Me?" Sabrina exclaimed. "But what'll I tell those kids about Santa?"

"I don't know," Mr. Humbert replied. "Tell 'em he had to go to the North Pole to get ready to go on his midnight ride. Tell 'em he had to go fix a broken toy. Tell them he drank some bad eggnog—I don't care! Just get some smiles on those kids' faces before our buddy Hunter Chase here starts his cameras rolling and ruins the mall's reputation! I've got after-Christmas sales to worry about, and I don't need the bad press. Got it?"

Sabrina nodded, but she couldn't help but wonder if anybody was worrying about the kids in all this.

So Sabrina put on her best Christmas smile, straightened her jingly green hat, and hurried over to where the kids were waiting.

"Hi, kids, I'm Pixie, Santa's number-one elf, and I—"

"You don't look like an elf," one kid complained.

"I thought elves were boys," said a boy.

"And little," said a little girl.

"Nope, elves come in all shapes and sizes—just like people," Sabrina explained, doing her best to be cheerful despite the sinking feeling in the pit of her stomach. "Now, kids, Santa had to leave to get ready for tonight. Isn't that exciting? Do you all know what happens at midnight?"

"David Letterman reads his Top Ten list?" Hunter Chase called out, laughing heartily at his lame joke.

Sabrina shot him an angry look. "Nooo. At midnight Santa flies through the air with his reindeer and sleigh to bring toys to good little girls and boys all over the world."

"Not where we live," Dylan said.

96

Sabrina's snappy reply froze in her throat. She didn't know what to say. Would the kids at the orphanage be getting presents under the tree in the morning? Or were the Wish Tree presents all they'd get? She glanced toward the nice woman in the red coat for help, but she was busy at the back of the line with a kid who had dropped his lollipop on the floor and was crying because he still wanted to eat it.

Sabrina felt ashamed of herself. She had spent the last week whining about how unhappy she was even while lying in the sun in Hawaii. She'd zapped her room full of luxuries trying to make up for all the presents she thought she didn't get as a child.

But there had always been plenty of nice presents when she was little, and more important, warm, loving parents to tuck her into bed with her dreams on Christmas Eve. Even after her parents' divorce, they'd managed to make every holiday of the year special for her, and she always knew, no matter what, that her parents loved her.

These kids weren't so lucky.

"So where're the toys?" Hunter's cameraman called out around a mouthful of gum. "We don't have all night."

"Okay, okay," Sabrina said through a tight smile. "Hang on to your underwear!" She hurried over to the sleigh to get the bag of special Wish Tree toys.

The sleigh was empty.

No Santa's pack chock-full of toys.

No stuffed animals or dolls. No balls. No trikes.

97

Not even a candy cane.

Sabrina climbed into the sleigh and looked under the seat. No presents. She jumped out and dropped to her knees to search beneath the sleigh. Behind the reindeer. Under the sheet of cottony, fake snow.

No presents.

Nada.

Zip.

*Now what, Pixie?* Sabrina asked herself grimly. She got to her feet and hurried back to the kids, who were waiting expectantly for their toys. "Um, it looks like maybe Santa took the presents with him," she stuttered, trying to smile. "Um, probably for safekeeping."

She could see the look of disbelief growing on the children's faces. The nice woman in the red coat looked tired and shook her head.

*Oh, brother,* Sabrina thought. *Christmas couldn't get any worse than this.*

And then it did.

Hunter Chase smoothed back his perfectly styled blond hair as he shoved his way in front of her to stand next to the disappointed kids, just as the cameraman hoisted his camera onto his shoulder and began to shoot.

"Live from Westbridge Mall, this is Hunter Chase—Channel 5's 'Seen on the Scene' news-guy—on the scene of a major, developing story."

*Oh, no—please, no,* Sabrina moaned.

"I'm here with the children of the Westbridge Orphanage. They got here tonight after waiting hours in the snow when their bus broke down. And now, at last, they've made it to the Westbridge Mall, hoping for some tiny present from Santa.

"Just look at these faces," he went on, strolling past the kids in line, who were now making faces and waving at the camera. "Are they pitiful? Needy children whose only Christmas Eve wish was to meet Santa and receive one measly little Christmas present—and what happens?"

Hunter paused dramatically while the camera zoomed in on his face.

"The Wish Tree toys have been stolen!"

☆

# Chapter 9

☆

What kind of rat, what kind of Scrooge . . . what kind of *mean, nasty Grinch* would steal Wish Tree presents on Christmas Eve?" Hunter exclaimed, his voice choked with emotion.

But Sabrina could tell he was really delighted. His boring "soft-news" story had suddenly turned into a tearjerker crime story, complete with gypped orphans!

"Ladies and gentlemen, this is one of the cruelest Christmas crimes I've ever covered," Hunter managed to go on, alliteratively. Then he grabbed Sabrina's arm and stuffed the microphone into her face. "This is Trixie, Santa's elf. Tell us, Trixie, where's Santa?"

Sabrina was caught off guard. "Um, well, it's Pixie, actually, and he's—"

"We know, off feeding the reindeer." Hunter

shook his head in dramatic disgust as his camera-man went in for a close-up. "But seriously, Trixie, how could you let something like this happen—on Christmas Eve, of all nights?"

Now the cameraman zoomed in on Sabrina's shocked face. She didn't know what to say. *It's not my fault!* she wanted to shout. But all she could do was shrug helplessly.

So Hunter filled in the blank. "Obviously some-body wasn't minding the generous contributions made by the good folks of Westbridge to this wonderful cause. And now these children, these poor, disappointed little waifs, will have to go home empty-handed."

The little boy named Dylan at the front of the line jabbed the girl next to him and said, "This bites. See, Alina? I *told* you there was no Santa Claus."

Little Alina opened her mouth to say something. Her bottom lip trembled.

And then she burst into tears.

Of course, Hunter Chase got the whole thing on camera. "Back to you, Chuck," he said at last, and the live broadcast ended.

*This is awful!* Sabrina thought. *They're too little to think like that!* But what could she do?

"Listen, the chorus is getting ready to sing Christmas carols," Sabrina told the children. "Why don't you listen to the music while I go find Santa? One of the performers sings like Elvis."

Several of the kids moaned.

"Who is Elvis?" Dylan muttered.

"Can we go home now?" one tired-looking little girl asked the woman in the red coat.

Sabrina grabbed her empty treat basket and turned her back so she could zap it full of candy canes. "Hey, listen. Everyone gets a candy cane while Pixie goes to get Santa." She passed the basket to the lady in the red coat, then dashed off as fast as her pointy little elf shoes would let her.

Sabrina found a pay phone around the corner and quickly called her aunts.

"Hello?" Hilda answered.

Sabrina could hear Bing Crosby singing "White Christmas" in the background.

"Aunt Hilda!" she shouted over the music. "Quick! How do you find a fake Santa in a mall on Christmas Eve?"

"Is this a joke?" Hilda asked with a giggle. "I love holiday riddles. Now, wait, don't tell me. Let me guess. How do you find a fake Santa—"

"No, no, no!" Sabrina exclaimed. "It's not a joke! I mean really! Look, I can't explain, but this is urgent. The mall's hired Santa Claus has disappeared, and I've got to find him. Can you tell me what to do?"

"That's a tough one," Hilda said. "You can't file a missing persons report for at least twenty-four hours. But maybe—"

"What's going on?" Zelda asked, cutting in on the other phone. "Sabrina, are you all right?"

Sabrina groaned. "I'm fine. I just need to find the mall Santa right away. It's urgent!"

"Hmm. Do you have a lock of his hair?" Zelda asked. "An article of clothing—a red glove, perhaps?"

"Nothing," Sabrina said. "I never even met the guy."

"Hmm, too bad he's not the *real* Santa Claus," Zelda said with a sigh. "Then, being a magical personality, you could look him up in the index of your book of magic."

"I can't look up somebody who just *plays* Santa?" Sabrina asked hopefully.

"Nope, only the real thing."

"Great," Sabrina mumbled.

"I think there's only one thing to do," Zelda said.

"What?" Sabrina asked hopefully.

"Use your feet."

"My feet?" Sabrina said. "You mean like, click my heels together like Dorothy in *The Wizard of Oz?*"

Zelda chuckled. "No, I mean use your feet, literally. As in hoof it. Walk. Walk around the mall and look for him."

"Oh, great," Sabrina said. "That could take till New Year's."

"Maybe not," Zelda said, laughing. "Let me see if I can give you a little boost. Hold the phone near your feet."

Sabrina did, and her aunt sent a little spell over the phone lines.

"One step, two steps, three steps, pause—
Help Sabrina find her Santa Claus."

Sabrina felt a tingly jolt in her green elf shoes, then her feet began to walk off.

"Thanks, Aunt Zelda!" Sabrina yelled as the phone cord stretched to the limit. "See you later. . . ."

*Weird,* Sabrina thought as she let her feet carry her around the mall. She tried to make a left turn just to see what would happen, but her feet went the other way, as if they had a mind of their own.

Finally, they took her down a long, empty corridor and stopped in front of a janitor's closet.

"I guess this is our stop, huh?" she asked her feet.

She tried the door, but it wouldn't open. Quickly she zapped the lock, and the door swung open.

Santa lay on his side on the floor, with a dirty rag stuffed in his mouth.

"Are you all right?" Sabrina asked him as she knelt to untie the ropes. "What happened?"

"Mmmk-hmph wwag mmt mm mmy mmff!"

"Oh, yeah, you can't talk with a rag in your mouth. Sorry." Sabrina gently removed the rag from his mouth so he could answer.

The man took a deep breath and let it out slowly. "Thank you, my dear," he said in a deep but gentle voice.

Sabrina studied the man. He didn't look at all the way Jenny had described him. His blue eyes weren't bloodshot, but twinkled as if he knew a secret. And his beard looked great. "What happened?" she repeated.

"It was my fault, really," the Santa said sheepishly. "You see, the regular mall Santa was, er, indisposed—"

"You mean Mr. Thompkins?"

"Yes, that's right."

"What was wrong with him?"

"Let's just say he'd indulged a little too much in the medicinals," the man said politely. Sabrina admired the way the man was reluctant to rat on his co-worker, even if he was a jerk.

"Anyway, I had just arrived to fill in for him," the man explained. "But as I approached Santa Land, I was listening to that wonderful music—"

"You mean the chorus concert?" Sabrina asked.

"Yes, wasn't it lovely?" The old man's startling blue eyes twinkled. "I especially loved their lively rendition of 'Santa Claus Is Coming to Town.' It's one of my favorites, you know."

"Yeah, mine, too," Sabrina said as she helped Santa to his feet. She was a little surprised the man hadn't already been working some other mall or department store. He looked pretty good, for a mall Santa—kind of like that guy in the old black-and-white movie *Miracle on Thirty-fourth Street.*

As she helped brush the dirt from his red wool suit, she noticed it was clean and well-cut—and didn't smell like mothballs or cigarette smoke, like most of them did. He seemed to fill out the belly area of the suit all by himself, too—without the addition of stuffing or pillows—and yet he looked robust and full of energy, not out of shape, like most of the overweight guys who played the part. The old-fashioned aftershave he was wearing was a nice touch, too. It smelled kind of like Old Spice mixed with . . . cinnamon and ginger?

And that neat white beard of his . . .

Well, Sabrina couldn't help herself—she *had* to give it a little tug!

"Ouch!"

"Ooh, sorry."

"Oh, that's all right, my dear," the old guy said with a chuckle as he rubbed his chin. "I suppose I should be used to it by now. You'd be surprised how many youngsters feel the need to give it a strong yank to see if it's real. It does seem to reassure them."

"It's a nice one," Sabrina said politely.

"Why, thank you, dear."

"So you were saying—?"

"Oh, yes." The man picked up his red cap and put it on, adjusting it to a jaunty angle before tossing the tip with the white ball on the end to the side. "I was watching Harvey do his Elvis impersonation, and was quite astonished by it, really—I could almost imagine the real Elvis had returned just in time for Christmas. . . ."

Sabrina wondered briefly how the guy knew Harvey's name.

She guessed he must have heard it announced or something when Harvey got up to sing.

"Then these two men approached me," the man went on. "One tall and skinny and one a bit stocky, shorter than you. They were dressed as security guards, and said there was a problem that only I could handle. Well, I always like to help out whenever I can, so I followed them down this hallway. But in the blink of an eye, they grabbed me quite roughly and stuffed that foul rag in my mouth. Then they tied me up and shoved me to the floor. And there I lay—until you came along to save me."

"That's terrible!" Sabrina cried. "What creeps!"

"Exactly. Oh, I don't mind so much for myself," he added, and then his face showed the first flush of anger. "But then they stole those poor children's toys!"

"Well, come on," Sabrina said, looping her arm through his.

"Why, where are we going?" the old guy asked.

"There are a bunch of little kids out there who are about to lose faith in Christmas," Sabrina said. "We can't let that happen!"

The man cocked one snowy-white eyebrow. "But what can we do? What about the toys?"

"It's Christmas, Santa," Sabrina said as she led him down the deserted hall. "Just cross your fingers and hope for a miracle."

# Chapter 10

Sabrina peeked around the corner at Santa Land, at the children still waiting in line.

Alina was still crying.

Most of the kids looked miserable.

And Mrs. Simmons' eyes turned upward, as if asking for guidance in how to deal with the ruined Christmas Eve trip to the mall.

Sabrina cringed when she saw the look in Dylan's eyes—like a scrawny little dog who was used to getting kicked.

"Listen, Sabrina," the mall Santa said, "I'll just—"

"Don't worry," Sabrina interrupted, motioning to him to stay hidden. "Stay here; I've got an idea."

"But, really," the old man insisted, a droll smile tugging at his lips. "Perhaps I should explain to you—"

"That's okay," she answered politely but firmly. "I promise I'll back up your story when we talk to the cops. But really, the most important thing here is the kids. I gotta take care of them first."

The mall Santa shook his head. "You're a very sweet young lady," the man said. "But how can you possibly—?"

"Don't you worry," Sabrina said, patting the old guy on his rounded shoulder. "Just make sure you're here when I'm ready to hand out those toys."

The old guy looked at her with a half-smile, his blue eyes twinkling. And then he gave her a little bow. "Fine, then, Sabrina. I'll leave it all in your hands."

"Thanks." She flashed him a grateful smile. "Now, just stay out of sight for a few moments, okay?"

The old guy gave her a thumbs-up sign. "Go for it, Sabrina dear."

"Back in five minutes!" she said cheerfully. Then she hurried toward Santa Land and—

*Snap!*

The entire mall—including this Santa guy—froze.

Time stood still.

Well, not really. Everywhere else in the world things continued according to mortal clocks. But for the mobs at the mall, everything had ground to a halt.

At first Sabrina considered searching for the two

crooks to get the stolen toys—but then quickly decided against it. They could be anywhere. And though she could probably look up a spell in her book of magic to track them down, who knew how long that could take? Right now, the kids were the most important thing.

So, instead, she ran as quickly as her jingling little pointed elf shoes would allow to the line of children at Santa Land.

With a snap of her fingers, a long scroll-like shopping list hovered in the air, accompanied by a quill pen and a bottle of ink. She walked past the long line of kids, touching each child gently on the top of the head, as if they were playing Duck, Duck, Goose. Then she uttered a quick spell:

> *"Trikes, and dolls, and games, and fishes,*
> *Reveal to me their Christmas wishes."*

Okay, so not that many kids wished for *fishes* at Christmas, but it was the only thing she could think of in a hurry that rhymed with *wishes*.

The scroll followed her down the line as she listened, the quill pen poised to write down every name and toy.

Sabrina was surprised as she heard the children's wishes.

Sure, there were wishes for the latest So-Sue-Me fashion doll, the hottest Monster Warriors from Planet Zed action figures, and the latest movie tie-in characters. She even heard one wish for a pony.

But, most of all, the kids wished for something that neither money, nor witchcraft, could buy.

*"I wish someone would adopt me so I could have Christmas in a real home. . . ."*

*"I wish Santa would bring me a doll—it's okay if she's not the prettiest or the most expensive—so I could hold her and love her and kiss her tears away . . . and tell her all my secrets. . . ."*

*"I wish Mrs. Whitefelder at the orphanage would learn to cook better. . . ."*

*"I wish I had a mommy and daddy. . . ."*

A lump formed in Sabrina's throat.

She understood how these kids felt. Really, she did.

Didn't she wish for the very same thing?

The difference was that she knew she'd see her parents again one day.

Who knew what the future held for these kids?

☆

# Chapter 11

☆

**E**xcuse me, sir." Sabrina lifted the hands of the janitor from his floor buffer and leaned the statue-like man against the wall. "I'll bring this right back."

Then she jumped on, revved the motor, and flew several feet into the air.

Brooms were so old-fashioned, and pretty uncomfortable, and his vacuum cleaner seemed to have a broken fan belt. She wished she had her vacuum cleaner from home. But the buffer would have to do.

After all, she had an awful lot of shopping to do. And while the crowds in the mall were in suspended animation, Christmas Eve in the rest of the world was still ticking away.

Sabrina zoomed—rather, whirred—around the mall, checking out what the hottest toys were, getting specifications and ideas. Toy Town was full of ideas, and soon she began zapping the bag full of wonderful toys.

Witches couldn't do brand-name toys, of course, but Sabrina made sure her toys were just as good——even better. In fact, these toys would have something none of the ordinary toys from the mall had: a label that read MADE AT THE NORTH POLE.

Sabrina realized she was having a ball. Being an only child, she didn't have any younger brothers or sisters to shop for—but this was almost as good.

Just think how delighted the kids would be.

She even whipped up a nice gift set of bubble bath and perfumed body lotion for Mrs. Simmons. She figured the woman could use a few moments of escape after taking care of so many restless kids at the mall on Christmas Eve!

At last Sabrina headed back to the janitor, buffing a long stretch of floor on her landing as a thankyou for borrowing the equipment. As soon as she'd propped the janitor back on the handle, she raced back to the deserted hallway where her Santa was waiting.

"Let's see now . . ." She checked the bag to make sure she had something for everyone. To make each gift extra special, she zapped the children's names on their gifts in a scraggly, old-fashioned handwriting that she thought looked like Santa's, so they'd know the present had been chosen especially for them.

Sabrina started to close up the bag, then stopped.

She remembered all their wishes.

Of course, she couldn't bring back parents or find new people to adopt them. She wouldn't dare do anything to try to meddle in their lives that way— since *terrrrrrrrrible* things might happen as an unexpected result. But she could do something.

She whirled her hand over Santa's sack, wrapping each present with something invisible to the eye.

"A big warm hug . . ."

Sniff!

Sabrina looked around. She thought she'd heard a sniffle, but how could she? Everyone was still frozen in place. Behind her, the mall Santa stood as still and as silent as the stuffed one in the toy store window.

But the toys weren't enough. Sabrina wondered how she could make this an extra-special Christmas Eve for those kids, one they would never forget.

"Got it!" She'd seen a miniature plastic toy sleigh with eight tiny reindeer in a gift shop on the corner, and now she floated it down the hallway and rested it on the floor in front of her.

Then she used a magnifying spell—*poof!*—

A full-size shiny red sleigh appeared. The eight living reindeer stamped their feet, and their hooves clattered on the polished mall floor. Their brushed coats gleamed under the bright mall lights, and jingle bells on their harnesses rang festively as they shook their heads.

"Whoo-hoo!" Sabrina hollered. "We're rockin'!"

Then with a quick *snap!* she unfroze everyone in the mall.

The mall Santa shook his head and gasped when he saw the bag of toys. "Sabrina! Did you catch the thieves?"

"Uh, no," she replied hastily, "but I did manage to round up some toys that I think will be perfect for our kids."

"Wonderful!" the old guy exclaimed, his eyes all aglow. "And what handsome reindeer," he added, running his hand along the lead's strong flank. "Wherever did you find them in Westbridge?"

Sabrina shrugged. "Let's just say I used a little Christmas magic."

The Santa winked. "That's the best kind!"

Then he and Sabrina climbed into the sleigh, and the mall Santa snapped the reins. "Now, Dasher! Now, Dancer! Now, Prancer and Vixen! On, Comet! On, Cupid! On, Donder and Blitzen!"

*Whoa, this guy is totally excellent!* Sabrina thought. She'd *never* seen a hired Santa who could remember *all eight* reindeer names—in order!

She couldn't resist. As the reindeer slowly pulled the flat, waxed runners of the old-fashioned sleigh toward Santa Land and the straggly line of sad-looking kids, she used a touch of magic to shower them with big, lacy snowflakes. The Santa guy looked up in amazement.

"Santa Land special effects," she explained.

"Nice touch," he commented, nodding in approval.

Dylan was the first to spot them. He whirled around at the first sound of the jingling sleigh bells, and his look of suspicion soon melted as a great big smile lit up his face.

"Look, everybody!" he shouted excitedly. "It's Santa Claus!"

The kids looked stunned at first, then began to laugh and squeal and cheer as the sleigh pulled up and stopped right in front of them.

"And look at those reindeer," Dylan said to Alina, whose tears had all dried. "They're *real!*" He gazed up at the mall Santa, who was smiling down in delight, and whispered, "See, everybody. It's the *real* Santa Claus, too! He *didn't* forget about us!"

Sabrina and Santa exchanged a look.

"Okay, Pixie!" Santa exclaimed. "Won't you please help these young people up to my lap? I just might have a few presents tucked away in my sleigh. Ho, ho, ho!"

*Gosh,* thought Sabrina, *the way he says it, it doesn't sound corny at all.*

Sabrina hopped down and helped each kid, one by one, to climb up into the sleigh. The old guy took his time with each child, chatting and sharing secrets and letting them hold the reins to the reindeer. Then he handed each one his or her own special present.

"Wow—you knew my name!" Alina exclaimed softly.

"Of course I know your name, Alina," the mall guy replied with a small hug. "Santa knows *everyone's* name."

Sabrina grinned in delight.

And Hunter Chase, the Channel 5 "Seen on the Scene" newsguy, got it all.

It was a busy time, and sometime during the whole thing Sabrina vaguely remembered hearing the chorus performing again, heard Harvey sing his solo. He sounded great, even though, she had to remind herself, it wasn't really him singing, it was really Elvis's voice. Part of her wished she could go watch, but she couldn't leave her kids.

At last they had handed out all the toys, and the mall Santa motioned to Mrs. Simmons to climb into the sleigh. Sabrina managed to "come up with" a few carrots and juicy red apples for the kids to feed the reindeer, while Santa handed Mrs. Simmons her present.

Sabrina hoped the woman would like what she'd gotten her. And she noticed that, although she still seemed tired, she was smiling now.

"Thank you for everything," Mrs. Simmons told Santa and Sabrina. "But I'd better get these kids back to the bus. I've got to get them fed and to bed."

Sabrina saw the mall Santa catch her by the arm. "Excuse me, madam, but might I recommend that you *not* stop by any fast-food establishments on the way home?"

"Oh, really? How come?"

"Because," he replied with a twinkle in his eye, "there's quite a Christmas Eve dinner awaiting you and the children when you get home—um, from me and the Westbridge cheerleaders' Wish Tree fund, of course."

*Huh?* Sabrina thought. *I didn't know the cheerleaders had arranged that. Maybe even Libby's Ice-Queen heart defrosted a little at Christmas.*

Mrs. Simmons couldn't help herself. She threw her arms around the mall Santa and hugged him. "Thanks, Santa. And Merry Christmas to you, too!"

With that, she hurried down from the sleigh and gathered up her kids like a flock of restless chickens. "Come on, kids. Bring your presents, now. We've got a surprise waiting for us back at the home."

"Really?" Alina said, her eyes shining. "I hope it's something good to eat."

And as they hurried toward the exit, Sabrina saw Dylan look back over his shoulder and wave at Santa. "You know something, Alina?" she heard him say. "This is the best Christmas I ever had!"

Sabrina had to agree.

Suddenly she realized how late it was. The mall was closing!

The mall Santa shook Sabrina's hand. "You did a good night's work tonight," he told her. "And I'm sure you made a lot of little kids happy. It was quite a joy to work with you, but now I must be off. It is my busiest night of the year, after all!"

Sabrina chuckled. Crazy old guy. She hoped the mall would use him again next year.

"Oh, hey, uh, Pixie . . . or whatever your name is." Mr. Humbert was over by the sleigh, scratching his head as he looked over the reindeer. "That was really terrific, what you and ol' Santa pulled off here with those kids."

"Why, thank you—"

"Yeah, Hunter Chase got it all," Mr. Humbert rushed on, not really listening to her. "It's going to be great public relations for the mall."

"Wonderful," Sabrina said dryly as she pulled off her green jingle bell hat.

"I think I owe you and Mr. Santa a bonus," he added.

"Oh, well, I was really just filling in for my friend, you know, so—"

"Whatever," Mr. Humbert interrupted. "So split it with her. Come by the office on Monday for your check, okay?"

"Sure, whatever." She started to walk away.

"But, hey, wait a minute!" Mr. Humbert cried. "What about these reindeer? You can't just leave 'em here. Where do they go?"

"Oops, sorry, I forgot." Sabrina patted the front reindeer affectionately on the nose. "Don't worry. I'll see that they get home."

"Great," Mr. Humbert said. "Well, thanks again. I've got to go close up the office. Merry Christmas!"

"Yeah, you, too." Sabrina gave the reindeer a pat on the cheek, and then whispered in his ear. "Let's go find Harvey, guys. Maybe he'd enjoy an old-fashioned little sleigh ride home."

The reindeer snorted their approval.

But when Sabrina hurried toward the stage where the chorus had performed, she discovered that they had long since finished. The stage was empty.

Harvey—and just about everyone else in the mall—was already gone.

☆

# Chapter 12

☆

The mall was a pretty dismal place with no people. Just a place with a bunch of things piled up. "Merry Christmas," she said, and her voice echoed lonesomely down the hall.

Sabrina started to reverse the magnification spell and send the sleigh and reindeer back to the shop window. But then she changed her mind.

She left enough money to cover the purchase on the shop counter, then climbed up into the sleigh. She waved her hands in an "open sesame" kind of gesture, and the mall's two glass exit doors swung open.

Then, with a shake of the reins, she drove the eight beribboned reindeer and shining red sleigh outside into the cold, dark night.

*Very* cold night.

*Hmmm,* she thought. *Maybe I was a little too hasty in ditching that Hawaii thing. . . .*

Nah. The frosty air definitely felt Christmasy.

And though she hadn't exactly gotten her wish—since it wasn't actually snowing—there was enough snow left on the ground from the previous snowstorm to technically call it a white Christmas.

The parking lot was nearly deserted, and the streetlights sparkled on patches of snow. There were a few cars driving by on the streets, but most people were settled somewhere—at parties, or celebrating with families, or tucking little children into bed.

"Giddyap!" she shouted, flicking the reins, and the reindeer trotted down the snowy street toward home. It wasn't *exactly* the evening she'd imagined, but it was still a beautiful night for a sleigh ride.

"Mommy, look!" Sabrina heard a little boy shout.

Sabrina realized she was still wearing her funny green Pixie suit, and must look pretty weird, dashing through the snow in an old-fashioned open sleigh drawn by eight reindeer in the middle of Westbridge.

On Christmas Eve.

But the little boy's shopped-till-she-was-about-to-drop mommy didn't even look up. "Yes, dear, now get in the car. It's late and we've got to get home. I still have a million presents to wrap."

*What a terrible way to spend Christmas Eve,* Sabrina thought. Giving presents shouldn't be a chore.

Once in the small, faded blue hatchback car, the little boy pressed his nose against the glass and waved as they drove off. Sabrina waved back until they disappeared into the night. Then, with a snap, she changed back into her regular clothes and warm, black boots.

Sabrina liked the way the snow muffled ordinary sounds, and for a while the only sound on the street was of reindeer hooves and jingle bells and the soft swoosh of the waxed runners on snow.

*I wonder if Jenny is having a good time with her family,* Sabrina thought.

*I wonder if Libby is having "The Perfect Christmas" with her family. . . .*

And then—

*I wonder where Harvey is. . . .*

With a sigh, she glanced up at the bright stars, sparkling like diamonds scattered across the black-velvet sky, and wondered if her parents— off somewhere in Peru and coughing under the $Q$'s—were thinking of her. "Merry Christmas, Mom and Dad," she murmured. "Wherever you are . . ."

She should be feeling blue . . . but even though Harvey had forgotten their plans to meet after the chorus concert, she realized that, somehow, she didn't.

She smiled. She'd had fun being Pixie. And it was really nice to give those kids at the mall something special for Christmas Eve—a little surprise, a little fantasy, a little Christmas magic.

Funny, but in spite of everything, it was one of the best Christmas Eves she'd ever had.

*Maybe it was because you stopped thinking about yourself for a few minutes,* she gently scolded herself. Trying to do something nice for those kids had helped her forget about her own troubles, which really weren't much at all.

Suddenly the sleigh began to tremble. The reindeer seemed agitated. And then—

Her ride home turned back into a miniature sleigh and eight tiny reindeer.

And Sabrina landed on her backside in the slush.

"Okay, Cinderella, time to hoof it," she said as she scrambled to her feet. She picked up the tiny plastic sleigh and slipped it into her pocket. It would be a nice souvenir to remind her of tonight. She could put it on the shelf next to her snow-dome.

Sabrina headed for home, her black boots crunching in the snow.

At the street corner, she whirled around nervously when she thought she heard something.

"Meo-o-o-w!"

A black cat crossed her path in the moonlight.

"Salem!" Sabrina exclaimed. "What are you

doing out here? I thought you hated taking walks. Especially with snow on the ground."

"Checking the quick marts for extra eggnog?" the black cat quipped.

Sabrina chuckled. "Now, *that* I can almost believe."

"Actually, Hilda and Zelda were a little worried about you. Mind you, I wasn't, I *never* worry—except when the stock market plunges. Anyway, I thought I should—I mean they sent me out to walk you home."

"That's so nice," she said, and bent to scratch him behind the ears.

*"Yowl!"* Salem complained. "Your hands are like ice!"

"Yeah, yeah, I know," Sabrina said, stuffing her hands into the warm pockets of her down coat. "I keep meaning to get some gloves."

"So, get some," Salem said with a shrug.

Sabrina blinked twice, then smiled. "Okay. Got 'em." She pulled her hands from her pockets and held them up in front of her face. "Ugh! Pea green? *Not* my color tonight." She blinked, and they transformed into a rich, black chenille pair, accented with black fur cuffs.

"Ah, my favorite color," Salem said, then gasped. "But hey, what's with the fur?"

"Don't worry, Salem. I *only* wear *fake.*"

"Good girl," Salem purred.

As they strolled home through the cold night,

Sabrina told Salem everything that had happened at the mall, including how someone had stolen the children's toys.

"Those dogs!" Salem snarled. "Even I, in all my dreams of world domination, never once took advantage of little kids."

"Yeah, it was really lame."

"So, where's Harvey?" Salem wanted to know.

Sabrina glanced around. "Um, he had plans."

"I know. But I thought those plans were with *you*," Salem persisted.

"Okay, okay, we did have plans, but they sort of fell through," Sabrina said. "Can we not talk about it?"

"Sorry," Salem said. "Didn't mean to get your back up. So, what about these crooks?"

"What about them?"

"What did you do to them?"

"Nothing," Sabrina admitted. "I guess they got away."

"Got away?" Salem exclaimed. "From a *witch?*"

"Hmm. Good point." Sabrina paced back and forth in the snow. "There ought to be an easy way to wrap a couple of creepy thieves and put them under the tree—at the police station."

"*Now* you're talking!" Salem followed Sabrina's pacing, his long, black tail twitching in excitement.

First Sabrina snapped a city map into her hands. Then she snapped a pen-sized Geiger counter into her hand, but set it on "Creep." She scanned it over the paper till it beeped.

"Bywood Road," Salem said. "That's not far from here. Come on."

They ran the few blocks to Bywood Road, then stopped to catch their breath.

"Look, Salem!" Sabrina whispered, pointing toward a broken-down van. "It's the two guys who tried to sell me a half-dead Christmas tree last week. Wow, these guys are kings of the cheap scam. But how do I know they're the ones who took our toys?"

The tall crook opened the back of the van and seemed to search for something. Fuming, he tossed a huge bag to the ground.

A few wallets and a couple of toys fell out.

The Wish Tree toys.

"There's your proof," Salem said.

"I'm calling the police!" Sabrina whispered. She snapped her fingers, and a cellular phone appeared in her hand.

"No, wait!" Salem laid a soft black paw on her dialing finger. "I've got a better idea."

"Oh, yeah? Like what?" she teased. "Are you going to pounce on them? Claw them? Knock 'em out with your tuna breath?"

"Hardly." Salem's whiskers twitched. "Just watch."

With an ear-piercing yowl, the black cat streaked across the street toward the crooks, then stopped and did what black cats do best.

He crossed their path.

"Yikes!" the short one muttered. "Hey, Vinnie, l-look. A black cat!"

"Yeah, yeah, Merle, so what?" the tall, skinny Vinnie replied.

"So, it's bad luck, that's what," Merle gasped.

"Like we don't already got bad luck?" Vinnie snapped. "Forget the cat, Merle, and help me find the jack so I can fix this flat tire!"

"I don't know, Vinnie, maybe we should—"

"Merle!" Vinnie hollered. "Get over here, *now!*"

"Better do as he says," Salem said, in a voice so low only Merle could hear.

Merle's eyes bugged out as he stared at Salem. Shrieking, he bolted to hide behind Vinnie, clutching at his arms, trembling as he stared back at Salem. "Th-th-that cat . . ."

"What is it now?" Vinnie snapped.

"Th-th-that cat! It—*talked* to me," Merle squeaked.

Vinnie rolled his eyes and yanked his arm loose. "Cats only talk on cartoons, you dolt. Now, cut it out. I ain't got time for this. We're going to get caught if we keep messing around."

Merle gulped and did as he was told.

Sabrina hissed at Salem, then whispered an idea.

Giggling, she watched as Salem sprang toward a snowman that stood in a yard, glistening in the moonlight beside a pile of forgotten snowballs.

Salem began to circle the snowman. Sabrina's breath formed little white puffs in the icy air as she chanted:

> "When yon black cat has
> circled thrice . . .

She liked that word—she remembered it from her father's last spell.

> "Bring to life the man
> made of snow and ice."

As soon as Salem finished his third circle, the snowman came to life.

"Uh, V-v-v-vin-nin-nin . . ." Merle stuttered.

"What is it now?" Vince snapped.

But Merle was so scared, he could only point.

Irritated, Vinnie turned around to bawl him out, then froze when he saw the snowman.

That's when Sabrina decided to give her snowman a little pitching practice. She zapped his tree-branch arms, and he began pelting the crooks with snowballs.

The two crooks freaked and started to run. The last Sabrina and Salem saw of them, the snowman was chasing them off into the night.

Sabrina and Salem slapped each other a high five.

"That was really fun!" Salem said, "but my toes

are cold now. Do you think you could carry me for a while?"

Laughing, Sabrina scooped Salem into her arms and hurried toward home.

But when they got to 133 Collins Road, Sabrina gasped in shock! She couldn't believe her eyes!

# Chapter 13

☆

☆

"Whatdya think?" Salem purred.

"Oh, Salem, it's beautiful!" Sabrina breathed.

Her aunts had totally transformed the old Victorian home, and this time they'd gotten it just right—without one watt of neon anywhere.

A trio of white candles burned in each of the old Victorian home's many windows. Evergreen garlands draped the railing of the wide porch, and a wreath tied up with an old-fashioned red velvet bow graced the front door.

The curving sidewalk was lined with glowing luminarias—made from flickering candles stuck into sand in plain white paper bags. As Sabrina hurried up the walk to the front porch, she caught a snowflake on her tongue. So what if this was the only house in town where it was snowing?

The smell of cinnamon welcomed her as she quietly eased open the front door.

Her aunts were decorating a tall, fat Fraser fir—by hand.

"Quit eating the popcorn, Hilda," she heard Zelda scold, "or there won't be any left for the tree."

And above the crackling fireplace hung a red velvet stocking with a crooked, white satin *S* appliquéd on the body.

"My stocking!" she cried, bursting into the room. Her mother had made it for her when she was six. The *S* bunched a little, and the stitches were a bit crooked—hey, her mom wasn't a seamstress—but that just made it even more special.

"Sabrina—you're home!" Aunt Zelda exclaimed.

"What do you think?" Hilda asked tentatively. "Did we do all right this time?"

"Oh, it's just perfect!" Sabrina said. "But where did you find this?" she asked, holding the stocking.

"We called your father," Hilda explained. "He got some old things out of storage and sent them to us. And he sent these, too."

She held open an old cardboard dress box filled with ornaments. Sabrina lifted one out. It was a crooked star, cut from red construction paper, that she'd decorated with glitter and strung on a string of yarn. She'd made it for her mom and dad in preschool—she couldn't believe they'd kept it. In fact, it looked like they'd saved everything. There was the Rudolph she'd made out of clay and painted. And the replica of her third-grade hand she'd made out of salt dough. And the satin red apple—for "the Big Apple"— that they'd bought on a trip to see the Macy's Thanksgiving Day parade in New York one year.

"Oh, these are so cool!" Sabrina said. "Can I put them on the tree?"

Zelda smiled and held up a star made of toothpicks stuck into a pine cone and sprayed silver. "That's what they're here for!"

Together they began to hang the treasured ornaments on the Fraser fir.

"I was a little worried about this at first," Zelda confessed as she examined their work. "I thought these might make you homesick for those Christmases you spent with your mom and dad."

Sabrina nodded as she hung up one of her favorites. A star picture frame made out of Popsicle sticks and painted red. A few grains of glitter still clung to the edges. And inside was a five-year-old Sabrina between her mom and dad. "They do in a way. But they also make me happy, too."

Impulsively she ran over and hugged both her aunts.

"Oh, and by the way, here's a present for you." Hilda held out a small box wrapped in the most beautiful gold paper she'd ever seen, with a huge red bow.

But before Sabrina could open it, the doorbell rang.

"I'll get it," Sabrina said as she hurried to the door.

Harvey.

He stood there in the porchlight, looking a little frozen, with snowflakes in his hair and his hands hidden behind his back.

"H'lo, Sabrina," he said shyly.

Sabrina was delighted to see him, but instead of saying so, she poked her head out the door and looked around. "So," she said, "where's your fan club?"

Harvey shrugged as a faint blush crossed his cheeks. "Gone. They only liked me for my voice—actually, Elvis's voice."

"Oh. Too bad."

"No, it's not," Harvey insisted. "Besides, you know crowds make me uncomfortable. I'm much better one-on-one. Besides, you're the only fan I really care about. And like the song says," he added shyly, "I'd have a blue Christmas without you."

Sabrina's smile told him how she felt.

"So, wanna come in?"

"Cool."

But he didn't. He just stood there.

"Um, Harvey?"

Harvey fidgeted a moment, then thrust a small wrapped package into her hands. "Merry Christmas, Sabrina."

Sabrina smiled down at the awkwardly wrapped package in her hands. She guessed he'd wrapped it himself.

"I guess you noticed that old paper bag I've been carrying around," he said as she tore off the paper. "I was making these for you, but I was afraid I wouldn't finish in time."

She opened the box. "Oh, gloves."

"I noticed how you seem to have cold hands a lot," Harvey explained, "so I made these for you— my mom taught me how to knit. But I had to hide it from my friends." He shrugged. "Some of the guys don't understand about knitting. Anyway, these are special."

Sabrina held them up. It was actually two pairs of gloves, except . . . two of the gloves had the fingers kind of knitted together. She looked up with a question in her eyes.

"That's so we can hold hands," Harvey explained.

"Oh, Harvey, how sweet." She gave him a quick hug.

Then he looked at her expectantly.

A gift! She hadn't gotten him anything else besides the Elvis voice, and she couldn't tell him

# Sabrina, the Teenage Witch

about that. She placed her hands behind her back and quickly zapped a wrapped package into them.

*But what do I put inside?* she thought frantically as she passed him the gift.

*Aftershave,* she thought as he pulled off the ribbon, and zapped a bottle into the package.

Nope, too boring.

*A flytying kit for making his own fishing lures!* she thought, zapping that into the package as he pulled off the paper. *But what if he doesn't like to fish?*

He was lifting off the lid.

This was her last chance. Hurry . . .

She blinked.

"Wow!" Harvey said, removing the gift. "It's just what I wanted."

Sabrina smiled. *Good gift,* she told herself. She'd given him something nobody else could give him.

A picture of her and Harvey in a nice frame.

"But I don't remember taking this picture," he said, a little puzzled.

"Um, I guess my aunts snapped it when we weren't looking," she said, then added quickly, "Now do you want to come in?"

Harvey grinned. "Cool."

Sabrina took him by the sleeve and pulled him into the house.

"Ah, just what we need," Aunt Zelda said as she greeted them. "A tall, young man to put the star on the tree."

As Harvey moved to help them, Sabrina sat on

the couch to open the gift Aunt Hilda had given her right before Harvey arrived.

"Salem," Sabrina said quietly, "Is this from you?"

"Nope," Salem said. "My present to you is under the tree—the one wrapped in the Garfield paper."

"Aunt Zelda, Aunt Hilda," Sabrina said slowly, "is this from you?"

"Oh, no, that's not from us," Aunt Zelda said. "A very nice gentleman brought it by about an hour ago. Said his name was Kris."

"Kris?" Sabrina said, puzzled. "I don't know any Kris."

"Really? That's odd," Zelda said. "Are you sure? He had this very distinguished-looking white beard and gorgeous blue eyes. Said he worked with you at the mall."

The Santa guy?!

"I guess I know who you mean." She caught Harvey's quizzical look and explained, "He was the mall Santa."

Harvey nodded. "I saw him. He was a good one. He looked real."

"He was kinda cute," Hilda added, handing Harvey a glass of eggnog. "I just loved the way his belly shook when he laughed like a bowl full of jelly. Didn't you, Zelda?"

"Yeah, he was a sweetheart. In fact, if he weren't so much younger than I . . ." Then she chuckled.

"But what am I thinking? He's married. Said he had to get going—or the missus would be waiting up all night for him."

Alone for a moment, Sabrina opened the unusual gift.

When she lifted off the lid, she stared in surprise.

Who was this guy?

It was the strangest gift she'd ever received. . . .

☆

# Chapter 14

☆

It was a snowdome.

But not just any snowdome.

It was *her* snowdome. The one her mother had given her. With the cheery cabin and the three evergreen trees.

How had the mall Santa gotten his hands on *that?*

And, more important, *why?*

Then she spotted a note inside, and quickly unfolded it to see what this crazy guy might have to say about all this.

Dear Sabrina,

Thank you for a marvelous Christmas Eve. You are truly one of Santa's *best* "little help-ers"! I'm sure the children of the Westbridge

Children's Home will never forget this night—thanks to you.

And so I wanted to thank *you* with a special gift.

Yes, I know this is your snowdome, and I know you must think I'm crazy, but just bear with me. Follow my instructions precisely.

Close your eyes and shake the snowdome three times—quickly—and without looking inside.

Then wait for the snow to settle.

Then see what you see.

Shake it again, and see what you see.

As many times as you like.

But only you will be able to see what you see.

> Merry Christmas!
> Love,
> Kris

See what you see? Only you will be able . . . ? Three times?

Oh, man, what a wacko, Sabrina thought.

But then . . .

She couldn't help herself.

She gave it a try.

She closed her eyes and shook the snowdome three times, quickly. She waited till she felt the snow would have settled.

*Okay, here goes. Open your eyes and you'll see the same old log cabin and three green evergreens that you always do.*

She opened her eyes—and gasped.

A lifelike image—like a small movie—played in the center of the dome. An image of three people . . .

And as the last flakes of snow settled, she couldn't believe her eyes.

It was her and her mom and her dad, from some Christmas past, opening presents on Christmas morning.

But how could that be?

She tried again, closing her eyes and shaking the dome, just as the letter had instructed.

And when she opened her eyes, another image appeared, of another holiday—the year her family had gone to New York and seen the Christmas parade. . . .

Again and again she tried it, and each time the snowdome revealed another image from her memory of happy holidays. Sometimes it was just Sabrina and her mother. Sometimes just her and her dad.

She hugged it to her chest. It was wonderful.

And then the last image she saw filled her with happiness. It was a Christmas in the future—she could tell because she seemed older, and so did her mom and dad. But they were together again, for Christmas, somewhere in the future.

She knew her parents would never get back together. They had their own lives and were very happy. Which is what she wanted for them.

But one day, sometime in the not-too-distant future, perhaps this promised that she'd share that special wonder of Christmas with them both again.

"Hey, what did you get?" Harvey asked, plopping down on the couch next to her.

"Uh, a snowdome," Sabrina said quickly.

"Oh, I love those things," Harvey said. "Can I see?" He took the snowdome before Sabrina could think up an excuse and flipped it over.

When the snow filtered down, Harvey looked surprised. "Whoa!"

"What! What do you see?" Sabrina asked worriedly. Could he see the startling movielike images from her Christmases past? How would she explain to him how they got inside a tiny glass snowdome?

He glanced at her with a funny look. "The same thing you do, I guess. That little log cabin with the three evergreen trees? Only it looks kind of like a cabin I dreamed up that I'd like to build up in the mountains one day. You know, a place to get away to, and do some skiing and reading."

"Oh, really?" Sabrina said in relief. "Sounds great."

*Only you will be able to see what you see. . . .*

Sabrina sat back, trying to take it all in.

That guy at the mall, the one who looked so

much like a real Santa . . . he couldn't be . . . could he?

But what other explanation could there be?

Suddenly Zelda, who was not a big television watcher, turned on the TV. "I hope you all don't mind. I think there's a Christmas special on with the three tenors."

"Cool," Harvey said. "Is that a new group?"

Zelda laughed. "I guess you could say that. It's the opera singers José Carreras, Placido Domingo, and Luciano Pavarotti singing Christmas carols."

"Oh, yeah, those guys," Harvey said, nodding.

But as she flipped through the channels, Sabrina spotted a familiar face. "Wait—look! It's Hunter Chase, the Channel 5 'Seen on the Scene' news-guy. He was at the mall."

They watched the quick clips of the Christmas concert:

A three-second shot of Libby doing her Christmas Cheer;

A four-second shot of the chorus, singing, "We Wish You a Merry—";

And a five-second shot of Harvey singing "Dreidel, Dreidel, Dreidel."

Harvey covered his face with a needlepoint Santa pillow.

"It's okay, Harvey, you can open your eyes now," Sabrina whispered. "It's all over."

"And now, this just in," Chuck Dahl, the anchor-man, said. "In a related story, there's been a strange new development in the Wish Tree toy robbery, which 'Seen on the Scene' first reported on our live broadcast earlier tonight. . . ."

Sabrina gulped. She and Salem exchanged a glance.

"The thieves have turned themselves in to the police," said anchorwoman Heather McKenzie, picking up the story. "And—get this—ranting about being chased by a raving snowman throwing snowballs!" Heather chuckled. "I guess someone's been drinking a little too much spiked eggnog tonight. Chuck?"

"Coming up next—tomorrow's weather with Skip Nelson."

Sabrina laughed and scooped Salem into her arms.

"Looks like we got 'em," Sabrina whispered into his ear.

"Too bad we don't have it on videotape," Salem snickered into her shoulder. "It would've been a Christmas classic."

Then they heard singing, but not from the TV. It was coming from their front yard.

Sabrina and her aunts hurried to the window and saw a huge group of carolers bundled up in colorful hats and scarves. Jenny waved happily from the middle of the group.

Sabrina, Harvey, and her aunts opened the front door to listen as they sang a few songs.

Then Jenny ran up on the porch.

"Are these all your relatives?" Sabrina asked in surprise.

"Well, most of them," Jenny said. "A few got snowed in coming down from Canada. But they might get here some time tomorrow." She gave Sabrina a quick hug. "I'm having so much fun. Thanks so much for filling in for me at the mall. I hope it wasn't too much trouble."

"Trouble?" Sabrina shook her head and laughed. "Nah, piece of cake."

Then Jenny ran back to join her family, and the carolers waved good-bye, singing "We Wish You a Merry Christmas" as they moved toward the next house.

Aunt Hilda and Aunt Zelda hurried inside to finish decorating, but Harvey grabbed Sabrina's sleeve. "It's a really pretty night. You want to sit out here a bit?"

"In the cold?"

Harvey shrugged. "We can try out your new gloves."

"Cool." Sabrina grinned. "Let me grab our coats."

Once they were zipped up, they laughed as they tried to figure out how to put on the gloves with the interlocking fingers. But at last they did, and they worked just fine.

Then they sat down on the porch steps, gazing at the moon and the starry sky.

Harvey was silent for a moment.

"Whatcha thinking?" Sabrina tried.

Harvey scratched his chin. "I was thinking how weird it is that it's only snowing over *your* house."

"Uh, yeah," Sabrina said nervously. "We'll have to ask Mr. Pool about that after winter break!" Then, to change the subject, she asked, "How was the concert?"

"I've decided I'm not gonna sing anymore," Harvey confided. "I'm going to stick to the bassoon. That way I can just enjoy making music, without having to worry about people watching me."

Then they spotted something . . . crossing the moon, a wisp of a cloud, or something.

"Hey, look at that cloud," Harvey said, pointing. "It almost looks like Santa and his reindeer."

Sabrina squinted. "Maybe it really is," she said softly.

Harvey laughed. "Yeah, maybe."

Sabrina thought about the year that was about to end, and the new year that was about to begin. Who knew what would happen?

But she could be sure of one thing. It was bound to be filled with magic—both the supernatural kind and the kind that happened to mortals sometimes when they weren't even looking.

Then she told Harvey about the kids at the mall. "I think I'm going to call Mrs. Simmons after Christmas and see if she needs any volunteers. You know, like, to be a big sister or something to some of the kids."

"Maybe they could use a big brother, too," Harvey said.

Sabrina smiled at him. "Yeah, I bet they could."

As Harvey squeezed her hand inside the crazy gloves, Sabrina realized that empty feeling inside her was gone.

And suddenly . . . it felt like Christmas.

Let Sabrina cast a spell on you in her next magical book . . .

## #6 Ben There, Done That

Uh-oh there's a witch with the hiccups in the house and that spells trouble! Sabrina's Aunt Hilda is afflicted with the hiccups and every time she hics something goes amiss. Hic! The fridge turns into a donkey. Hic! The sofa turns into a porch swing. Hic! You get the picture.

But then, Hilda goes one hiccup too far and the books for Sabrina's American History assignment disappear and one of the past presidents of the USA turns up in their place. Benjamin Franklin has been blasted from the 18th century into modern-day America and he seems to be enjoying the ride. He can't get enough of fast food, fast bikes, videos and liberated women . . . but Sabrina's convinced that, for the sake of the nation, she has to get him back to 1776 before the course of her life — and history — is changed forever.

Don't miss out on any of Sabrina's magical antics — conjure
up a book from the past for a truly spellbinding read . . .

# Sabrina
## The Teenage Witch™

## #4 Halloween Havoc

Halloween's here! Sabrina's going to throw a party to beat
all others. There's a monster movie theme and some fiendish
food to get everyone in the mood. Unfortunately,
'everyone' turns out to be Harvey and Jenny, everybody
else has blown Sabrina's party out in favour of Libby's
super-secret 'surprise' Halloween bash!

Sabrina's nose is put out of joint, but she doesn't have much
time for moping as her aunt Vesta takes the reigns and
invites some real horror-stories over to turn the night into a
truly monstrous success. The trouble is, Sabrina really
doesn't want her friends to find out about her witchy ways,
so she's got her work cut out keeping them from learning
the truth. Then, she discovers the magic pantry and a rather
persuasive young warlock, and Sabrina finds herself
creating some Halloween havoc of her own.

The trouble is, she may have started it, but she's got no idea
how to stop it and if she doesn't watch out, her carefully
constructed cover is about to be blown . . . for good!

# About the Author

CATHY EAST DUBOWSKI has written many books for children and young adults including *Sabrina, the Teenage Witch* titles *Fortune Cookie Fox* and *A Dog's Life*. Her husband, Mark, is a writer too and they have even been known to collaborate on some of their books.

Cathy writes in her office in a big red barn in North Carolina, where she lives with Mark, daughters Lauren and Megan, and their two golden retrievers, Macdougal and Morgan.

# Nancy Drew™

**Nancy Drew** Carolyn Keene
Runaway Bride

**Nancy Drew** Carolyn Keene
False Pretences

**Nancy Drew** Carolyn Keene
Out of Bounds

**Nancy Drew** Carolyn Keene
Making Waves

**Nancy Drew** Carolyn Keene
Illusions of Evil

**Nancy Drew** Carolyn Keene
Flirting with Danger

**Nancy Drew** Carolyn Keene
Fatal Attraction

**Nancy Drew** Carolyn Keene
Till Death Do Us Part

DROP DEAD